To my mom,
who taught me that any problem
can be solved with a little creativity

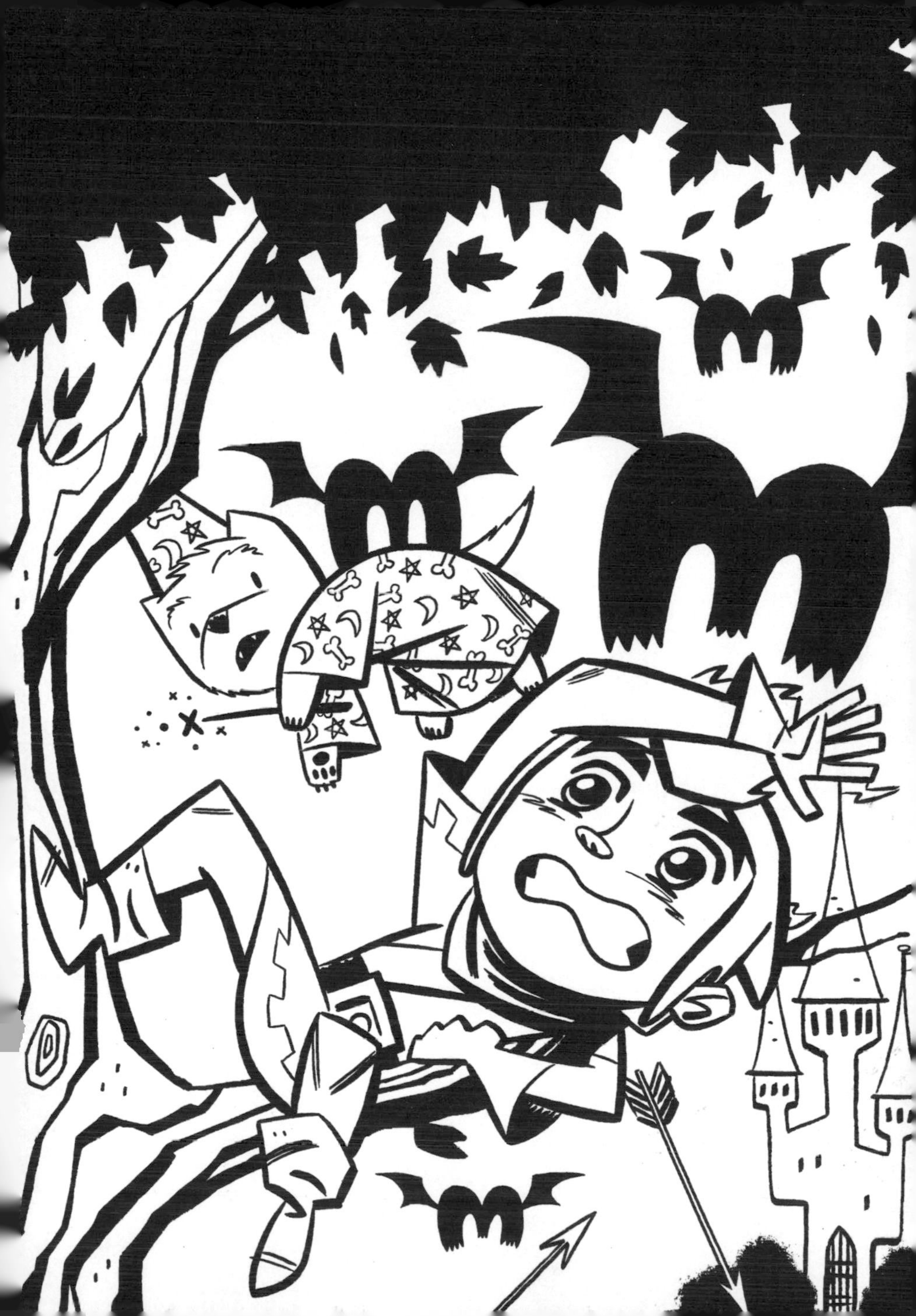

Also by Eric Wight

Frankie Pickle and the Closet of Doom

Frankie Pickle and the Pine Run 3000

FRANKIE PICKLE™
AND THE MATHEMATICAL MENACE

written and illustrated by
ERIC WIGHT

SIMON & SCHUSTER
BOOKS FOR YOUNG READERS
New York   London   Toronto   Sydney

SIMON & SCHUSTER BOOKS FOR YOUNG READERS
An imprint of Simon & Schuster Children's Publishing Division
1230 Avenue of the Americas, New York, New York 10020
This book is a work of fiction. Any references to historical events,
real people, or real locales are used fictitiously. Other names, characters,
places, and incidents are products of the author's imagination, and any
resemblance to actual events or locales or persons,
living or dead, is entirely coincidental.

SIMON & SCHUSTER BOOKS FOR YOUNG READERS is a
trademark of Simon & Schuster, Inc.
For information about special discounts for bulk purchases,
please contact Simon & Schuster Special Sales
at 1-866-506-1949 or business@simonandschuster.com.
The Simon & Schuster Speakers Bureau can bring authors to your live event.
For more information or to book an event, contact the Simon & Schuster Speakers Bureau
at 1-866-248-3049 or visit our website at www.simonspeakers.com.
Book design by Eric Wight and Tom Daly
The text for this book is set in Farao.
The illustrations for this book are rendered digitally.
Manufactured in the United States of America
0611 FFG
2 4 6 8 10 9 7 5 3 1
Library of Congress Cataloging-in-Publication Data
Wight, Eric, 1974–
Frankie Pickle and the mathematical menace / Eric Wight. — 1st ed.
p. cm.
Summary: Worried that he will not pass his math quiz on Monday,
Frankie cannot find any time to study over the weekend. Comic strip
illustrations are interspersed throughout the text.
ISBN 978-1-4169-8972-1 (hardcover : alk. paper)
[1. Examinations—Fiction. 2. Mathematics—Fiction. 3. Schools—Fiction.] I. Title.
PZ7.W6392Frd 2011
[Fic]—dc22
2010020801
ISBN 978-1-4391-5584-4 (eBook)

CHAPTER ONE

Frankie stared at the first question on his math quiz, and wrote down the number 23. That didn't seem right. He attacked it with his eraser, leaving behind a black smudge cloud. Maybe if he skipped ahead, the next problem would be easier to solve.

It wasn't. This one was even scarier. In fact, if Frankie turned his head sideways, the number 3 kind of looked like fangs.

He drew a pair of wings on it. Now it was a vampire bat! He added horns and claws and spiked tails to the other numbers.

Frankie's quiz was covered with number monsters! Better get rid of them before his teacher, Miss Gordon, found out. Biting down on the green metal end of his pencil, Frankie squeezed out every smidge of eraser he could. He went to work scrubbing

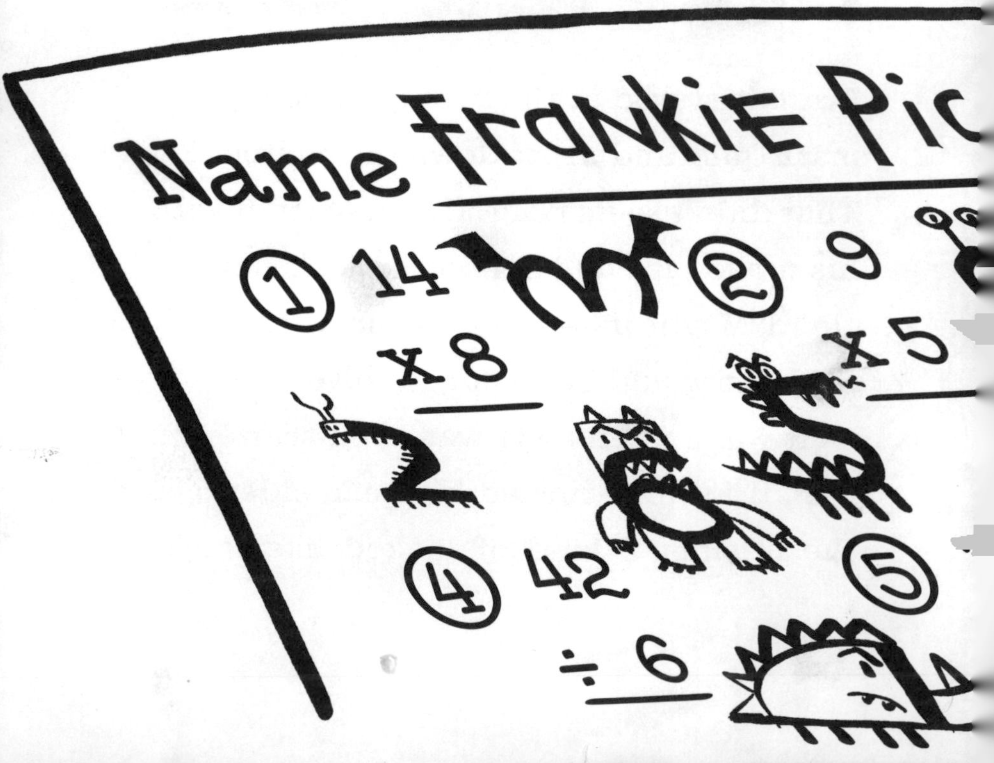

Name Frankie Pic
① 14
x 8
② 9
x 5
④ 42
÷ 6
⑤

an 8 with a Cyclops eye when his eraser—his ONLY eraser—popped out of the pencil, double-bounced across his desk, and rolled underneath Miss Gordon's chair.

These number monsters weren't going away without a fight.

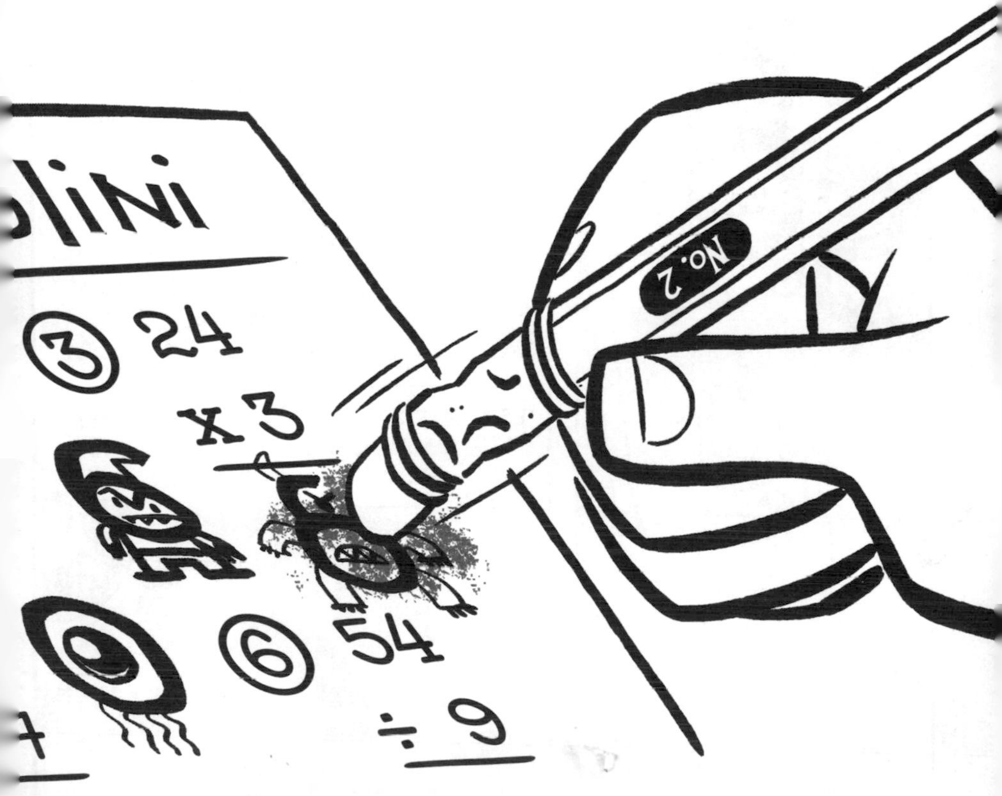
lini
③ 24
x3
⑥ 54
÷9
No. 2

CHAPTER TWO

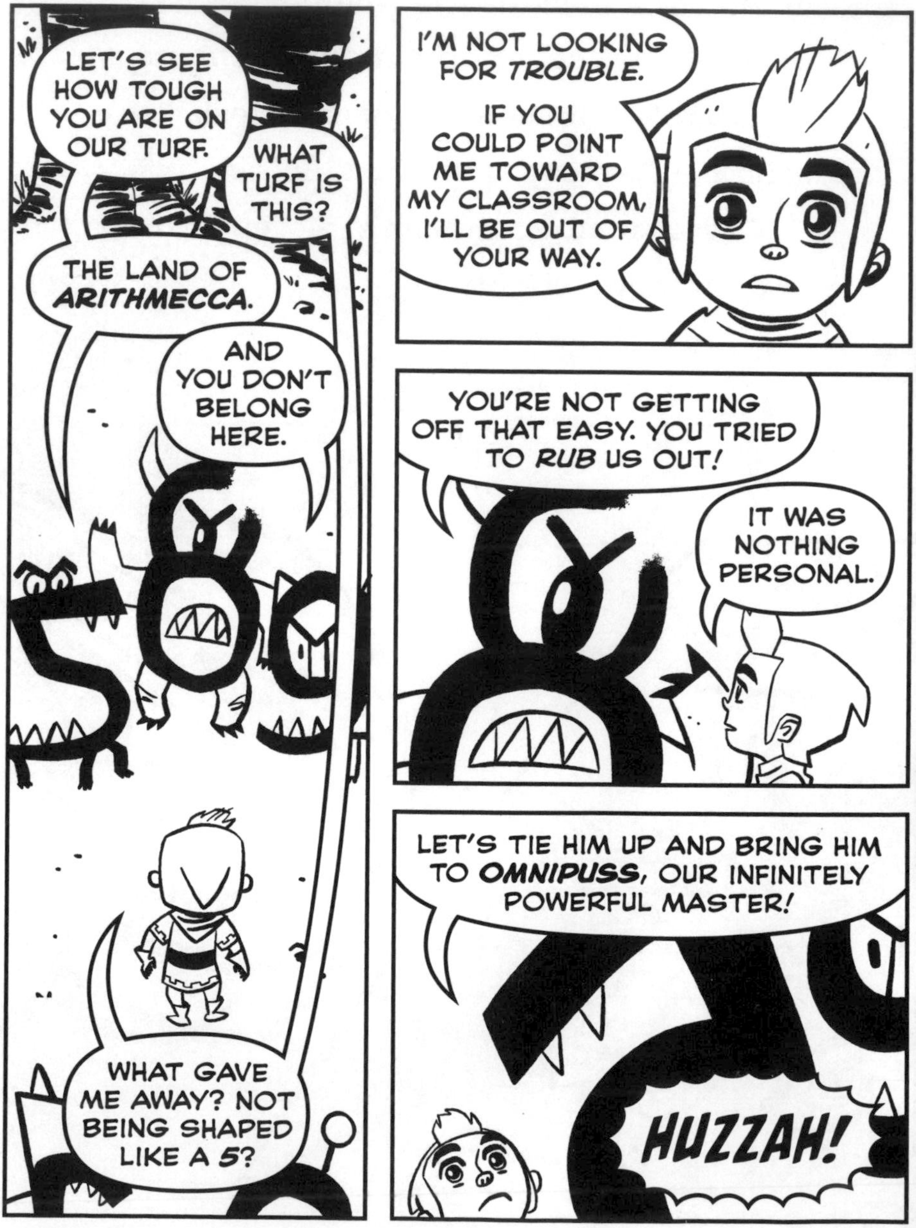
LET'S SEE HOW TOUGH YOU ARE ON OUR TURF.
WHAT TURF IS THIS?
THE LAND OF *ARITHMECCA*.
AND YOU DON'T BELONG HERE.
WHAT GAVE ME AWAY? NOT BEING SHAPED LIKE A *5*?
I'M NOT LOOKING FOR *TROUBLE*.
IF YOU COULD POINT ME TOWARD MY CLASSROOM, I'LL BE OUT OF YOUR WAY.
YOU'RE NOT GETTING OFF THAT EASY. YOU TRIED TO *RUB* US OUT!
IT WAS NOTHING PERSONAL.
LET'S TIE HIM UP AND BRING HIM TO ***OMNIPUSS***, OUR INFINITELY POWERFUL MASTER!
HUZZAH!

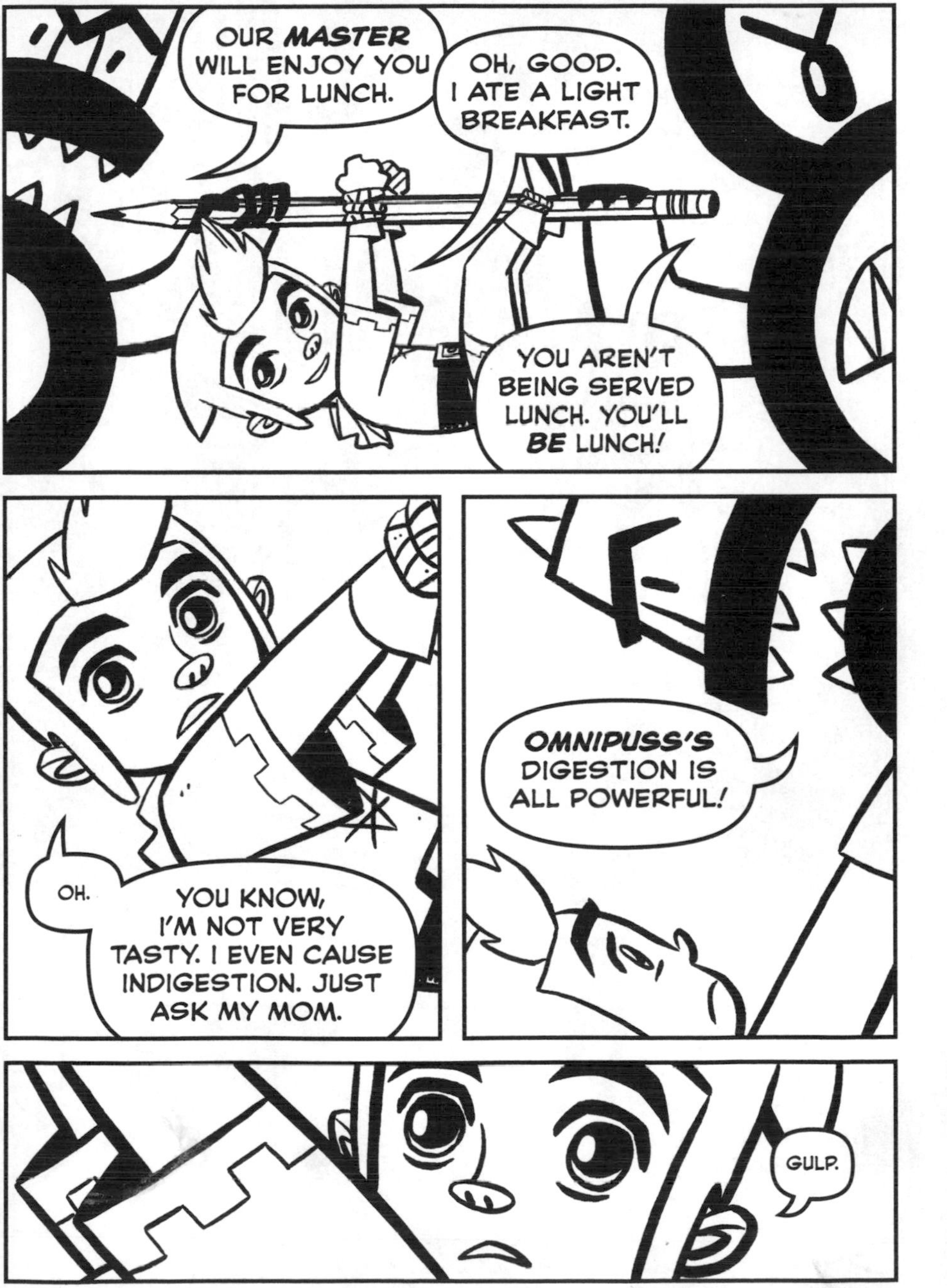
OUR MASTER WILL ENJOY YOU FOR LUNCH.
OH, GOOD. I ATE A LIGHT BREAKFAST.
YOU AREN'T BEING SERVED LUNCH. YOU'LL BE LUNCH!
OH.
YOU KNOW, I'M NOT VERY TASTY. I EVEN CAUSE INDIGESTION. JUST ASK MY MOM.
OMNIPUSS'S DIGESTION IS ALL POWERFUL!
GULP.

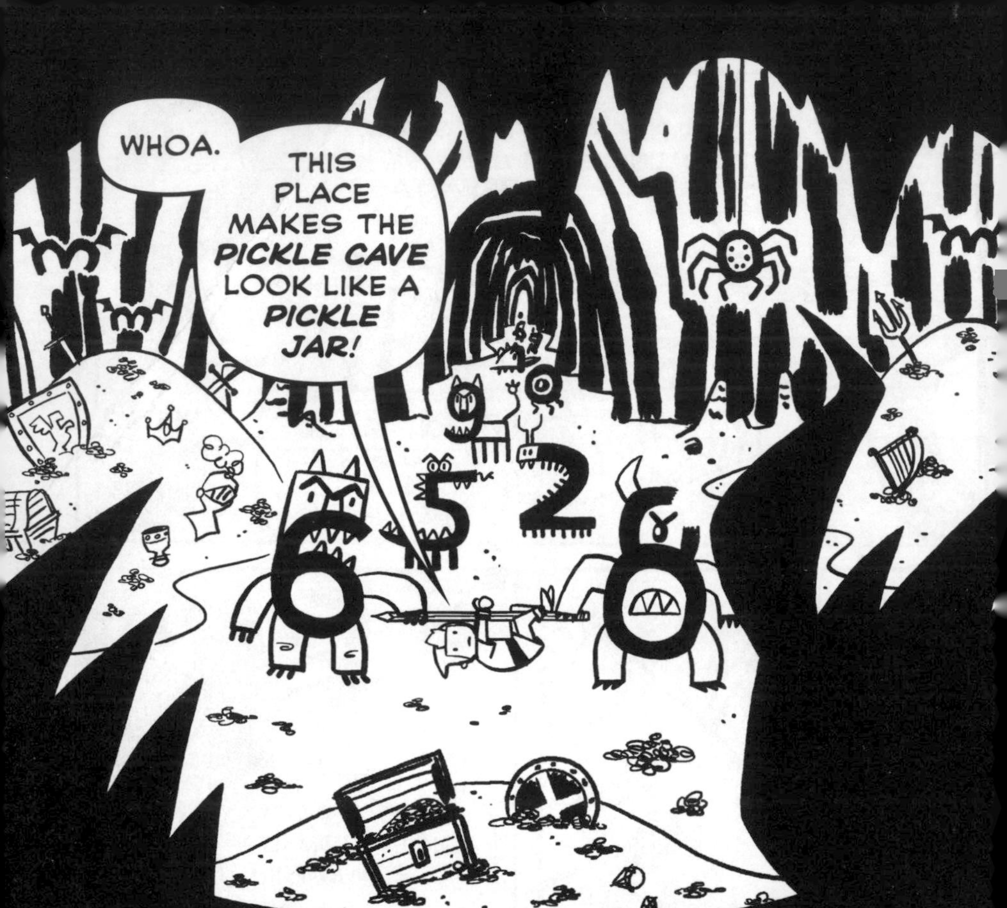
WHOA.
THIS PLACE MAKES THE *PICKLE CAVE* LOOK LIKE A *PICKLE JAR!*

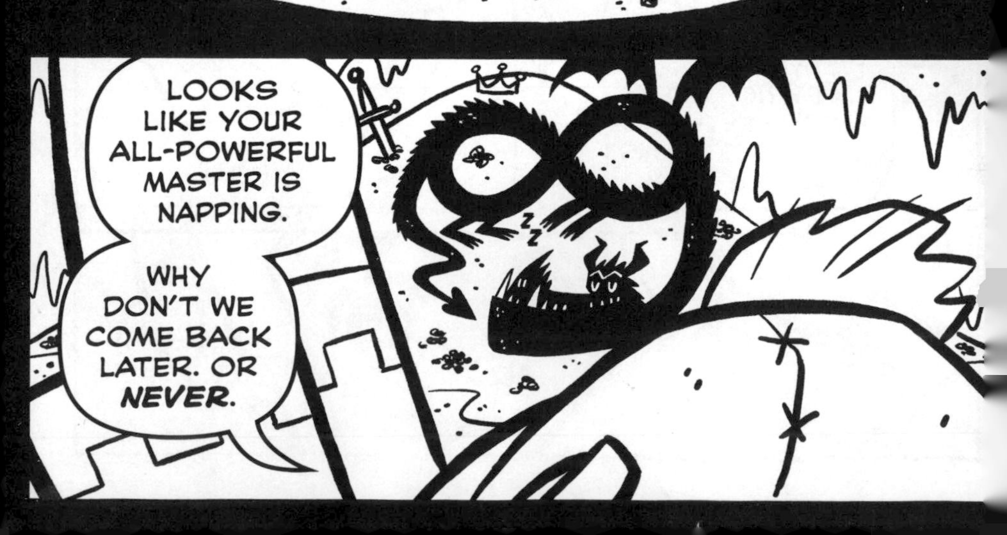
LOOKS LIKE YOUR ALL-POWERFUL MASTER IS NAPPING.
WHY DON'T WE COME BACK LATER. OR *NEVER.*
Z
Z
Z

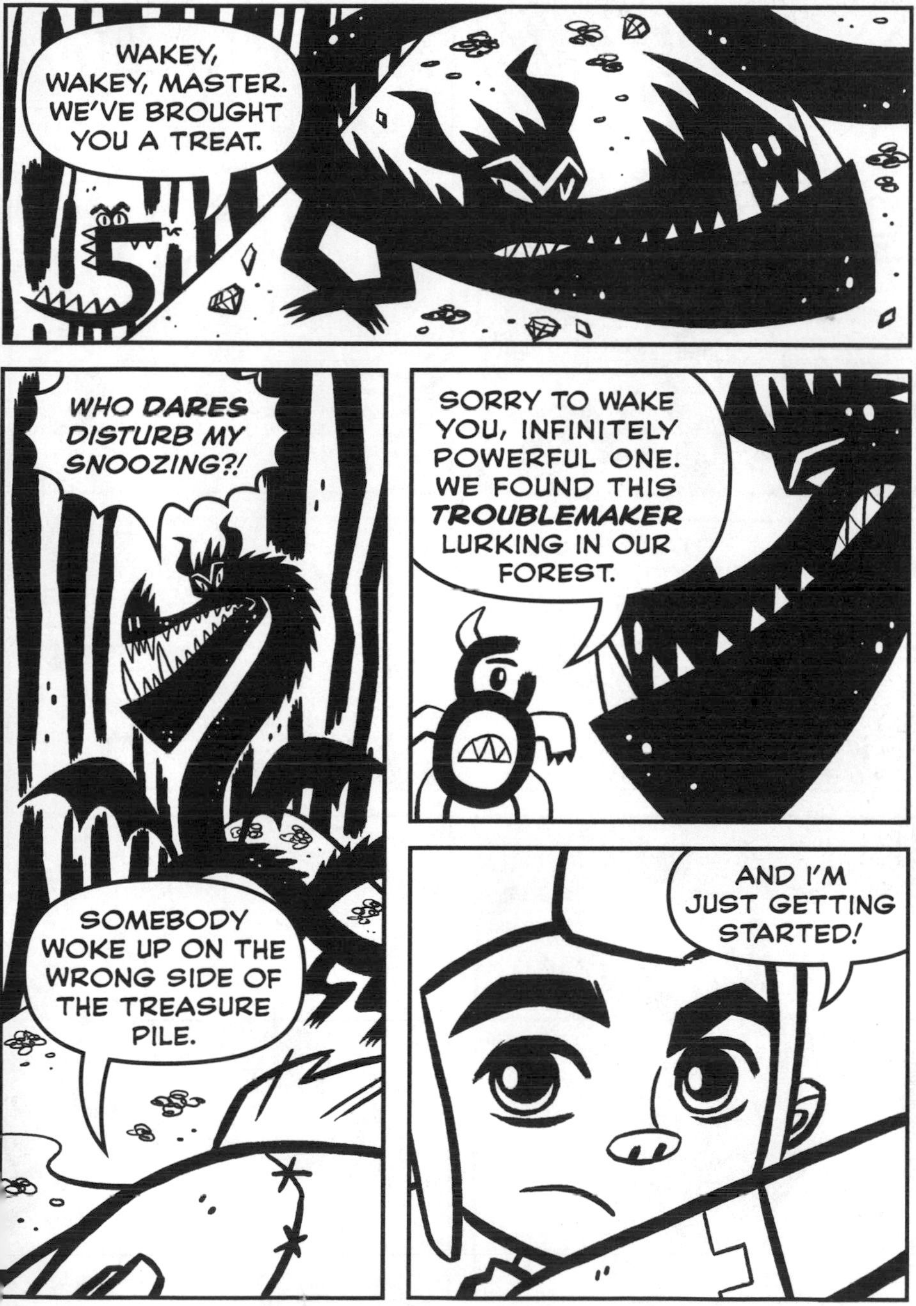
WAKEY, WAKEY, MASTER. WE'VE BROUGHT YOU A TREAT.
5
WHO DARES DISTURB MY SNOOZING?!
SORRY TO WAKE YOU, INFINITELY POWERFUL ONE. WE FOUND THIS TROUBLEMAKER LURKING IN OUR FOREST.
SOMEBODY WOKE UP ON THE WRONG SIDE OF THE TREASURE PILE.
AND I'M JUST GETTING STARTED!

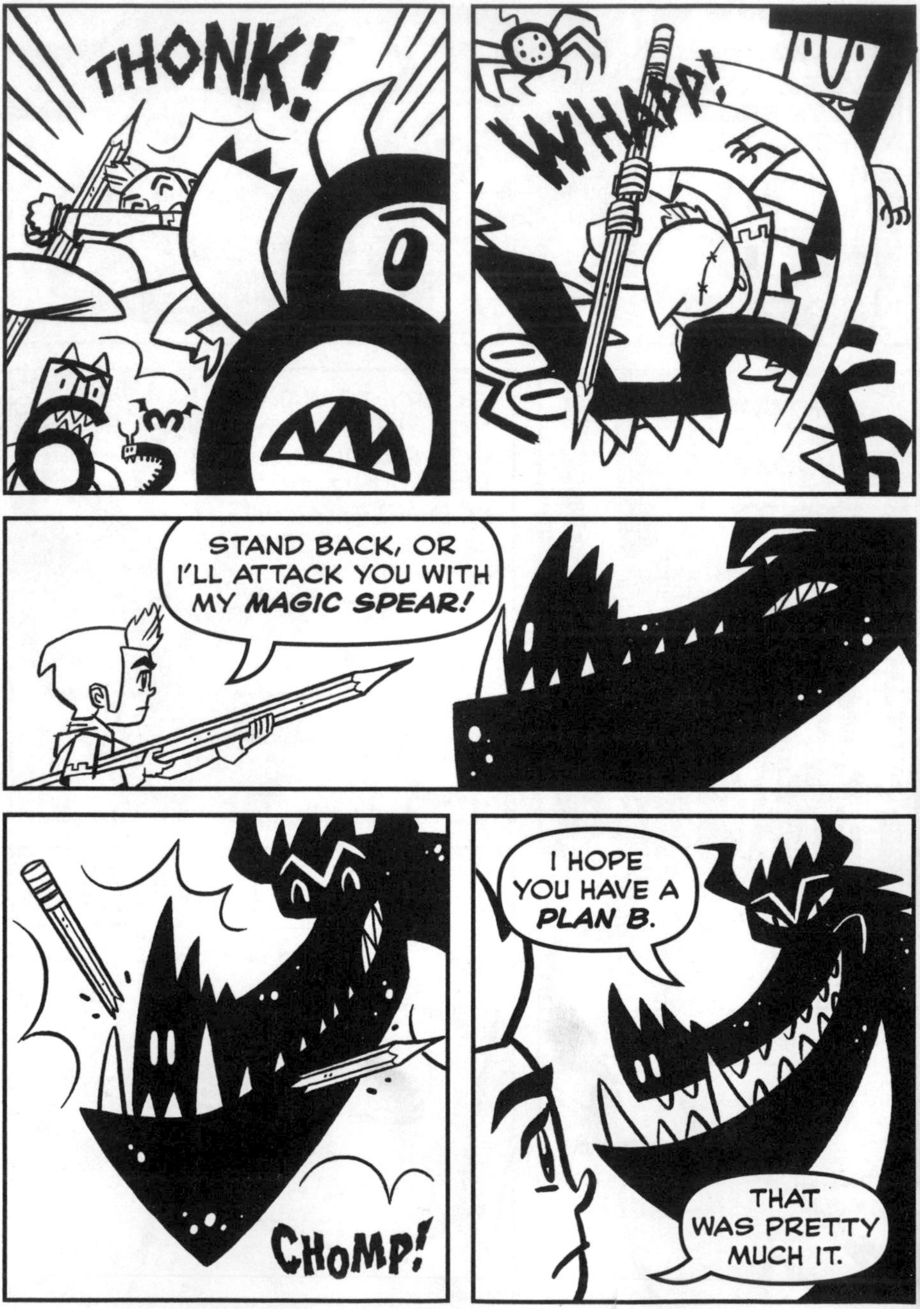
THONK!
WHAPP!
STAND BACK, OR I'LL ATTACK YOU WITH MY *MAGIC SPEAR!*
CHOMP!
I HOPE YOU HAVE A *PLAN B*.
THAT WAS PRETTY MUCH IT.

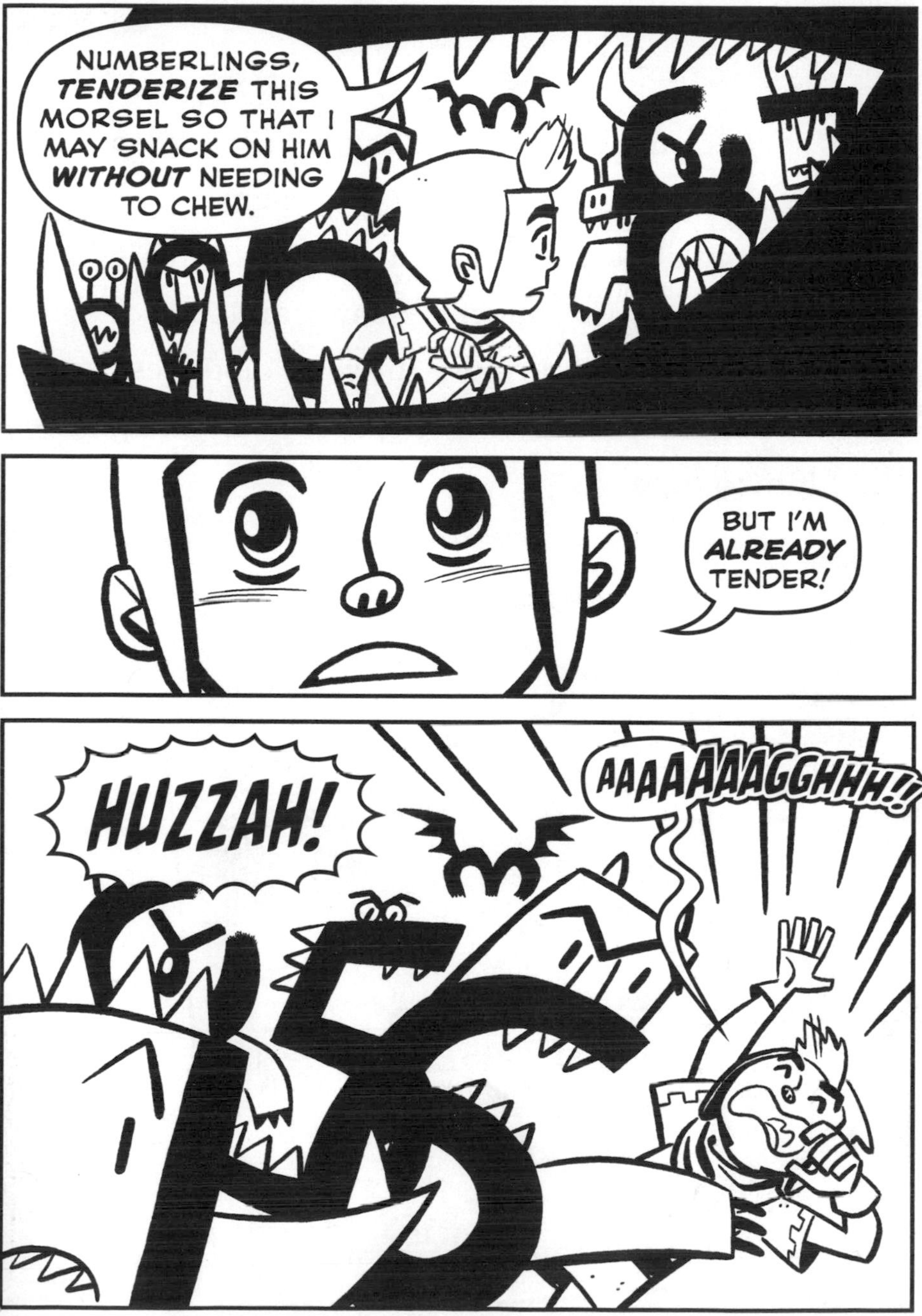
NUMBERLINGS, ***TENDERIZE*** THIS MORSEL SO THAT I MAY SNACK ON HIM ***WITHOUT*** NEEDING TO CHEW.
BUT I'M ***ALREADY*** TENDER!
HUZZAH!
AAAAAAAAGGHHH!!

"It's only the bell, Frankie," said Miss Gordon. "There's no need to scream."

Frankie calmed down. He was in his classroom. He hadn't been tenderized. Then he looked down at the scribbled mess of the math quiz Miss Gordon was asking him to turn in.

He wanted to scream again.

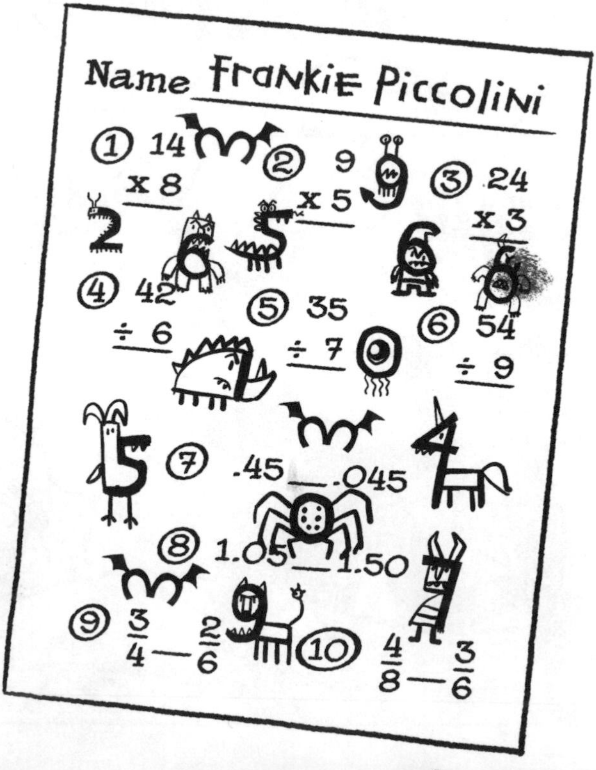

Name Frankie Piccolini
1 14 x 8
2 9 x 5
3 24 x 3
4 42 ÷ 6
5 35 ÷ 7
6 54 ÷ 9
7 .45 ___ .045
8 1.05 ___ 1.50
9 3/4 — 2/6
10 4/8 — 3/6

CHAPTER THREE

The following day at school was dreadful. Frankie had barely slept the night before. All he could think about was that math quiz. He was so tired at recess that he stayed frozen the entire time he played freeze tag. At least it was Friday. Only one more class until the weekend. Unfortunately, that class happened to be math. Maybe Frankie would get lucky and Miss

Gordon wouldn't have time to grade their quizzes until Monday.

"Good news, everyone," said Miss Gordon. "I had plenty of time last night to grade your quizzes."

Frankie groaned.

Miss Gordon flipped open a purple folder on her desk and said, "When I call your name, please come up and collect your paper."

Frankie squirmed in his seat. His hands were all sweaty. Waiting to hear his name was TORTURE.

But his name was never called. Weird. Maybe she forgot to grade it. Or lost it. Or maybe his monster doodles were so awesome, she wanted to keep it so it could be hung in a museum!

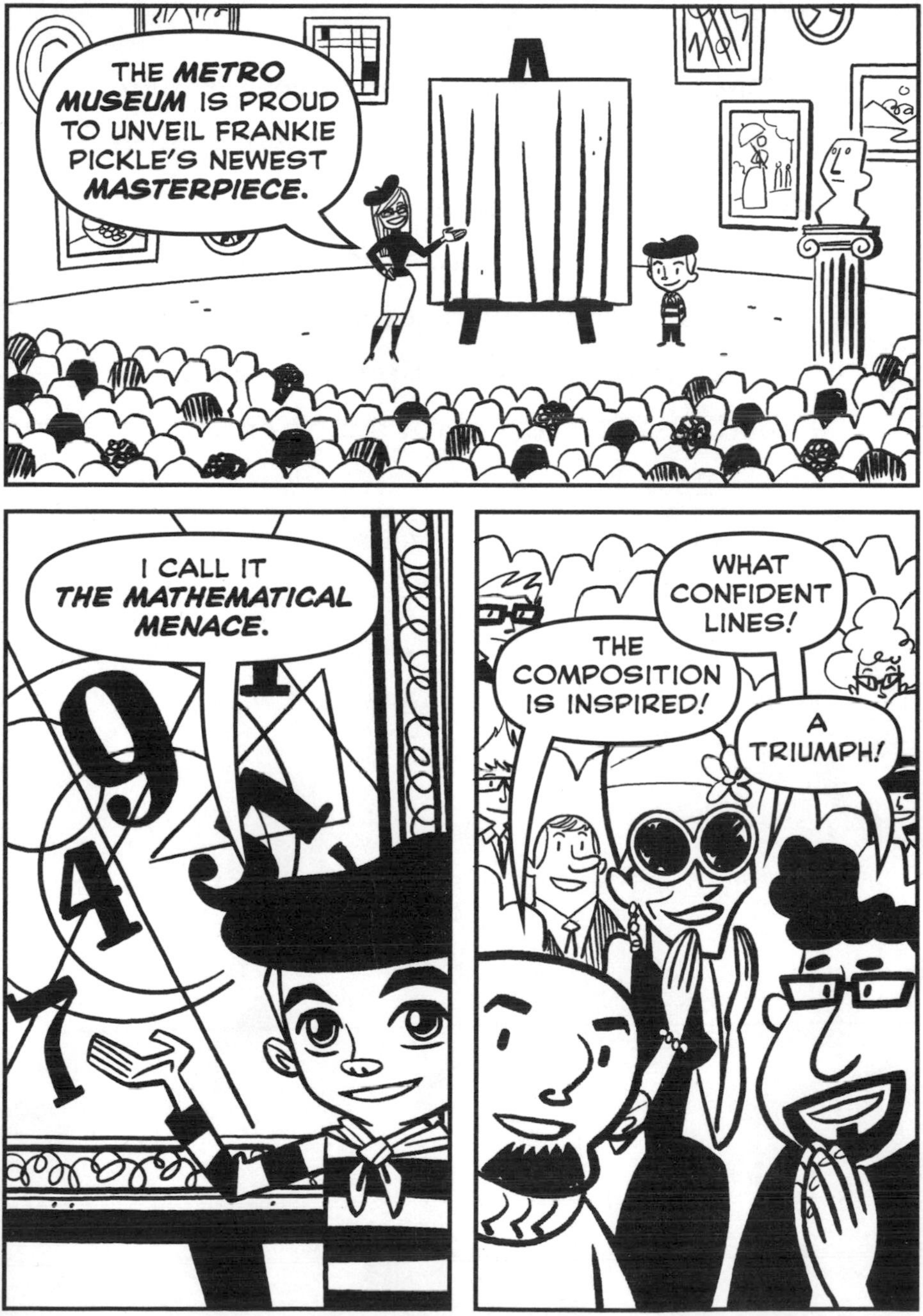
THE METRO MUSEUM IS PROUD TO UNVEIL FRANKIE PICKLE'S NEWEST MASTERPIECE.
I CALL IT THE MATHEMATICAL MENACE.
WHAT CONFIDENT LINES!
THE COMPOSITION IS INSPIRED!
A TRIUMPH!

The bell rang. School was over. Frankie couldn't believe it. Had he been spared from having to deal with his quiz? He packed up his things and began to file out of the room with the other kids.

That's when Miss Gordon said, "Frankie, I need to speak to you for a moment."

So close.

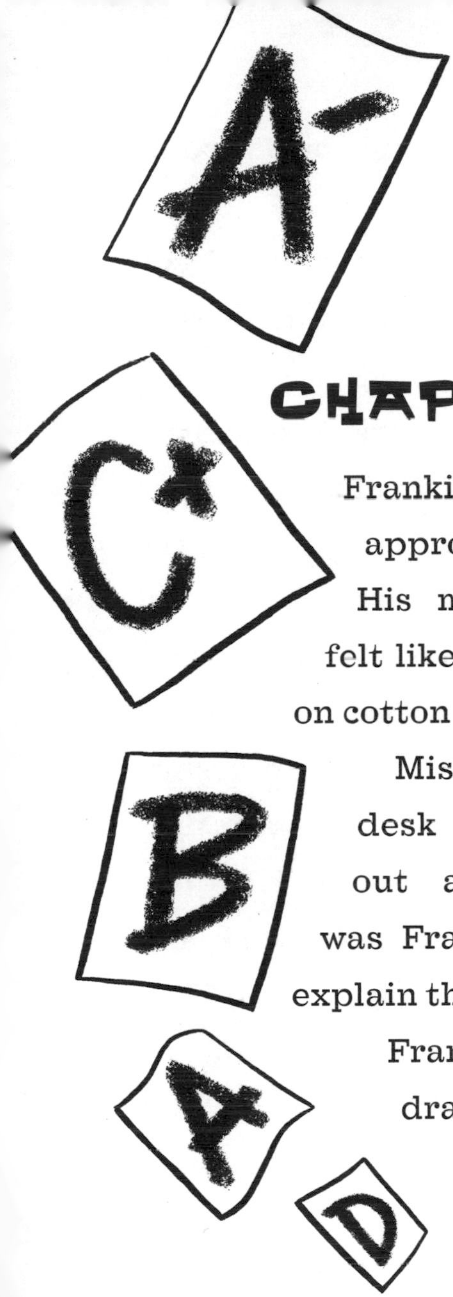

CHAPTER FOUR

Frankie turned and slowly approached Miss Gordon. His mouth was so dry, it felt like he had been snacking on cotton balls.

Miss Gordon opened her desk drawer and pulled out a red folder. Inside was Frankie's quiz. "Can you explain this to me?" she said.

Frankie looked at the drawings that covered his paper. "Well, the three is a vampire bat, the 9 is a snake monster, and the 8 is some kind of Cyclops."

"That's not what I meant. Why did you cover your quiz with drawings instead of solving the problems?"

"Oh," said Frankie. "I tried to answer them, but then I got stuck, and the numbers looked scary so I started adding the monster parts. I tried to erase them, but my pencil broke, and then class was over."

"I see," said Miss Gordon. "Here's the part I don't get." She removed an assortment of Frankie's old homework assignments from the same folder as his quiz. "You've done well with your homework, and you participate in class. Did you study?"

"Sure I did," said Frankie. During the whole bus ride to school to be exact. "But when I saw the quiz, my brain totally went blank."

"Hmmm . . ." Miss Gordon looked like she was trying to solve a math problem herself. "What if I gave you a second chance?"

"You can do that?"

"Considering that you didn't exactly take the quiz the first time, I think we can make an exception. Come see me Monday after school."

Frankie was so relieved, he could have done cartwheels down the hallway. But then he realized his "second chance" meant he was going to have to take his math quiz all over again. Now the only thing doing cartwheels was his stomach.

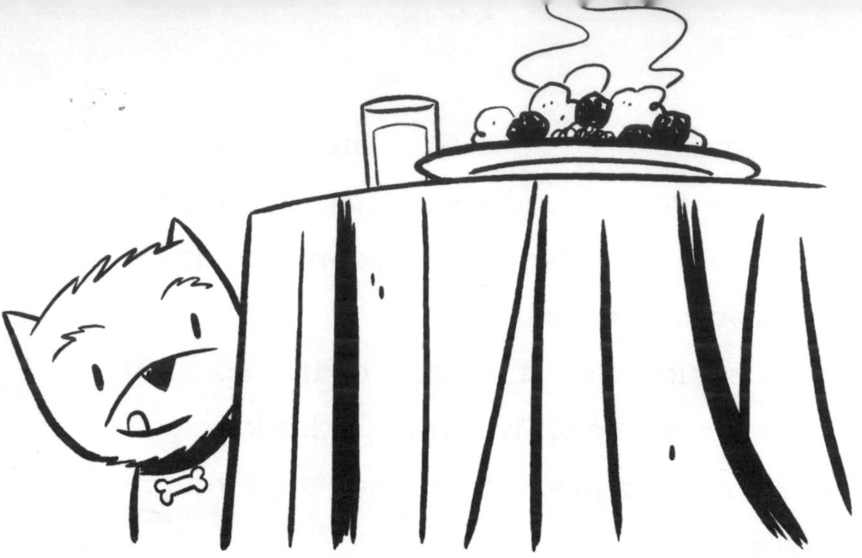

CHAPTER FIVE

Frankie sat at the dinner table, pushing meatballs around his plate. He didn't feel much like eating. All he could think about was having to take his math quiz all over again. Argyle sat patiently under Frankie's chair, hoping some food might drop on the floor.

"How'd you make out with your quiz yesterday?" said Dad.

Frankie dropped his fork. "What'd you

hear?" he said, his eyes darting back and forth between his parents.

They looked at each other curiously. "Should we have heard something?" said Mom.

"Oh . . . only that it was postponed until Monday."

"Postponed?" said Mom.

"Yeah . . . um . . . it's kind of a long story."

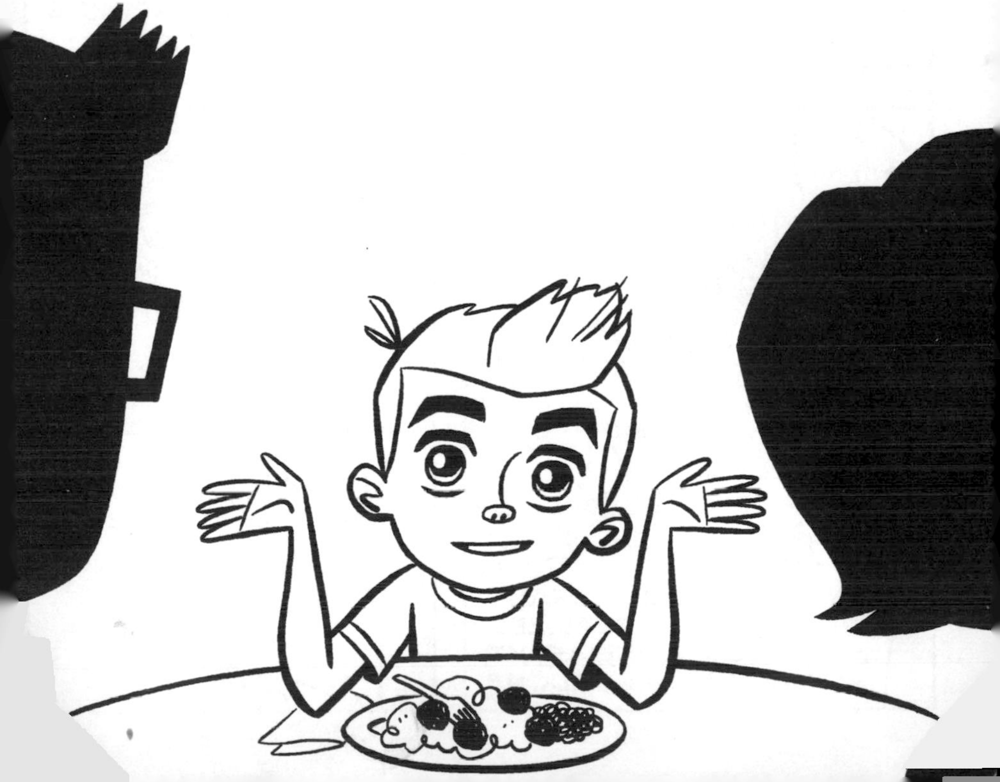

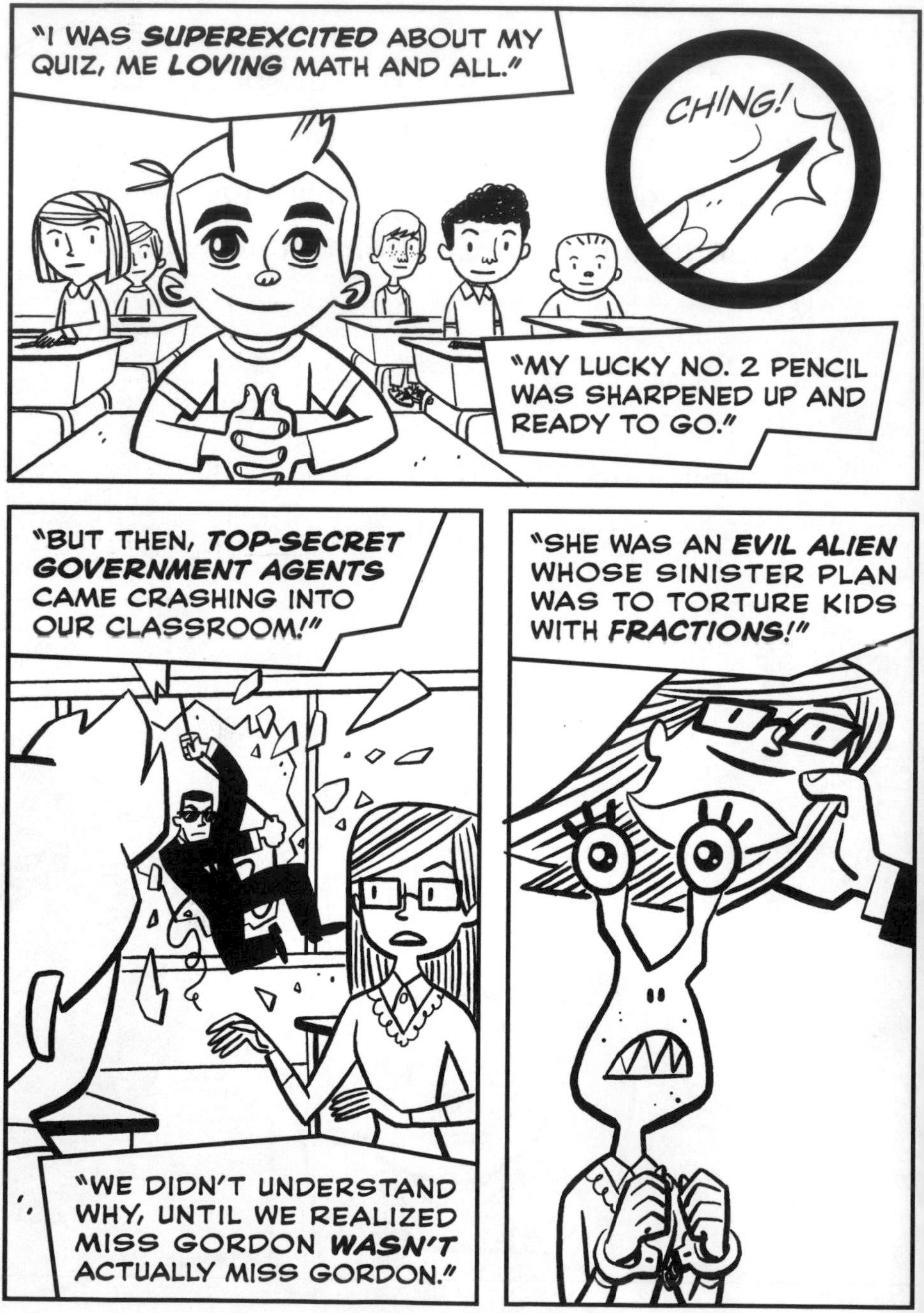
"I WAS SUPEREXCITED ABOUT MY QUIZ, ME LOVING MATH AND ALL."
CHING!
"MY LUCKY NO. 2 PENCIL WAS SHARPENED UP AND READY TO GO."
"BUT THEN, TOP-SECRET GOVERNMENT AGENTS CAME CRASHING INTO OUR CLASSROOM!"
"WE DIDN'T UNDERSTAND WHY, UNTIL WE REALIZED MISS GORDON WASN'T ACTUALLY MISS GORDON."
"SHE WAS AN EVIL ALIEN WHOSE SINISTER PLAN WAS TO TORTURE KIDS WITH FRACTIONS!"

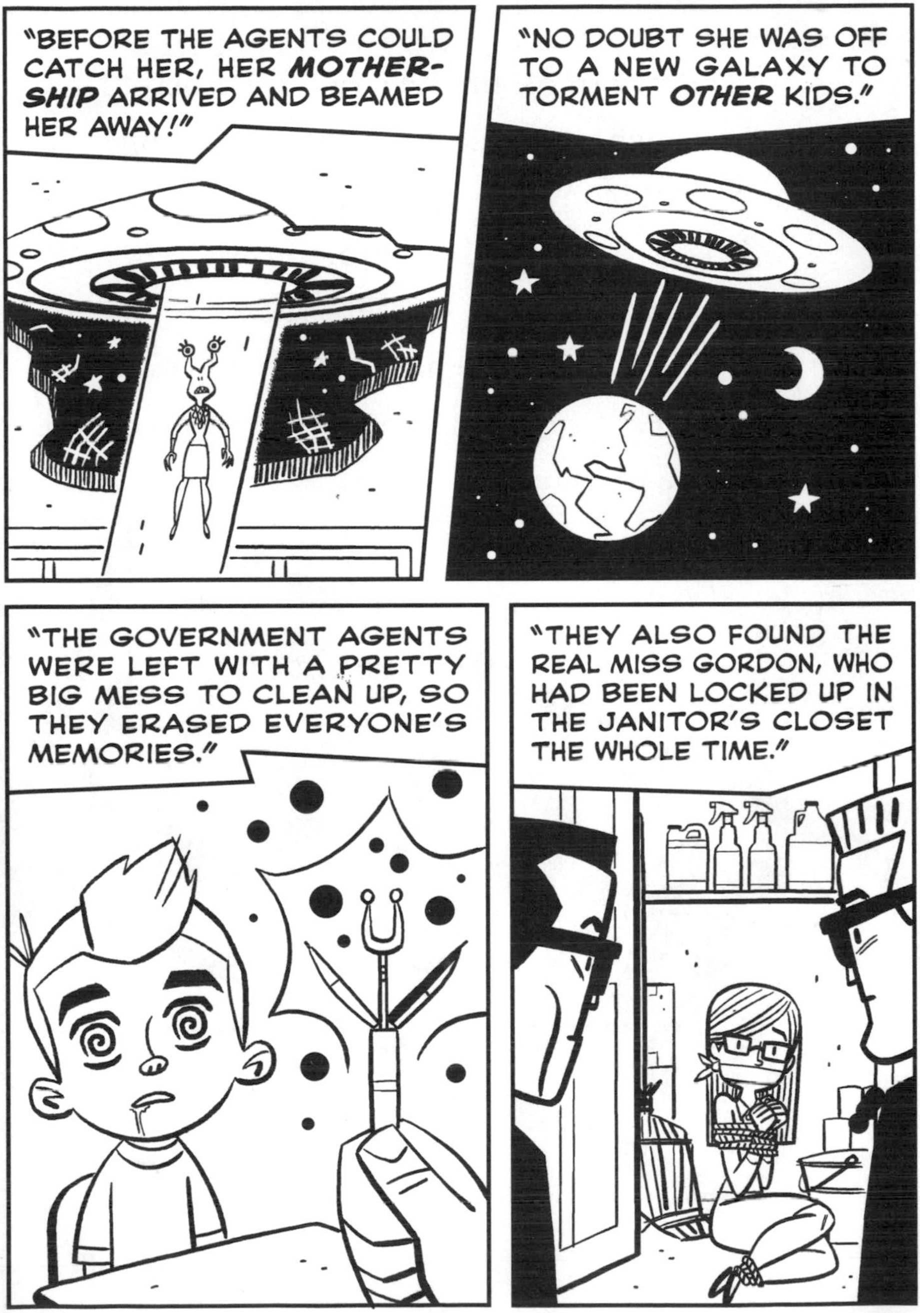
"BEFORE THE AGENTS COULD CATCH HER, HER ***MOTHER-SHIP*** ARRIVED AND BEAMED HER AWAY!"
"NO DOUBT SHE WAS OFF TO A NEW GALAXY TO TORMENT ***OTHER*** KIDS."
"THE GOVERNMENT AGENTS WERE LEFT WITH A PRETTY BIG MESS TO CLEAN UP, SO THEY ERASED EVERYONE'S MEMORIES."
"THEY ALSO FOUND THE REAL MISS GORDON, WHO HAD BEEN LOCKED UP IN THE JANITOR'S CLOSET THE WHOLE TIME."

"Because of all of the drama, Principal Kent thought it would be best to postpone class until Monday," said Frankie.

"That's a pretty incredible story," said Dad, trying to keep a straight face.

"It was so good, I'd like to hear it again," said Mom. "Only this time, without all of the made-up parts."

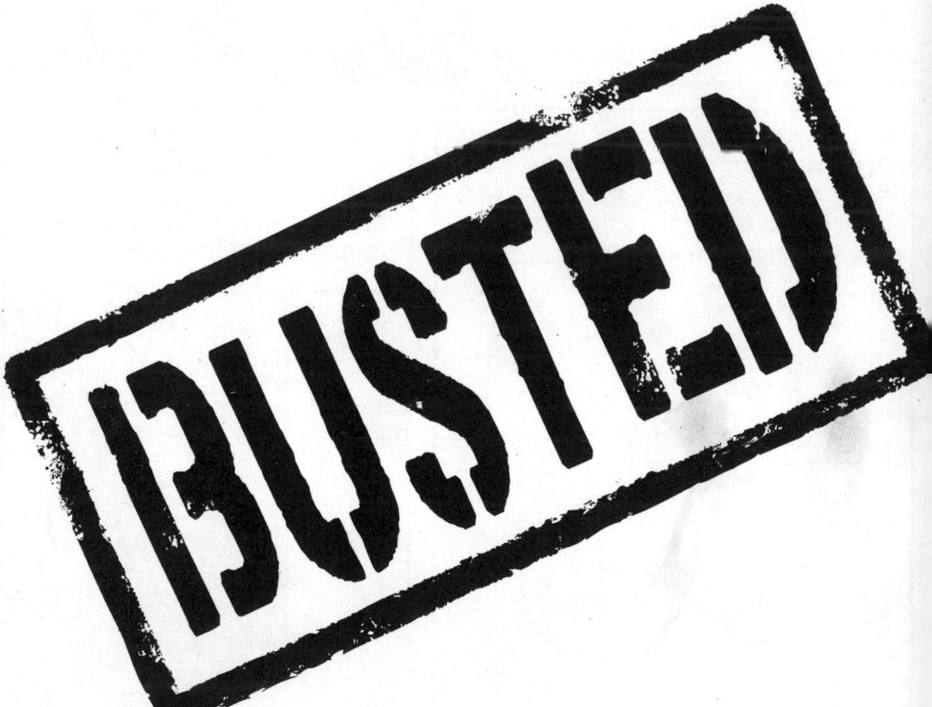
BUSTED

CHAPTER SIX

"A fire drill would have been way more believable," said Piper.

Mom gave her The Look. The one that scared ghosts.

Piper gulped. "*Or*...you should always tell the truth."

So Frankie told the truth. This time there were no aliens or secret government agents or even quizzes being canceled. The truth was that he couldn't finish a single math problem. Nada. Zilch. Zippo.

"Why didn't you just tell us that in the first place?" said Dad.

Frankie shrugged. "I didn't want to get into trouble."

"And how'd that work out?" said Mom.

Frankie smiled weakly. "That depends . . . Am I grounded?"

Mom and Dad looked at each other, then said at the same time, "No video games for a week."

"Then I guess not so good."

When asked why he thought he did so poorly, Frankie shrugged his shoulders. "Maybe math's not for me. No one can be good at everything."

"I am," said Piper.

Frankie wanted to argue with her, but she was right.

"Let's focus on the positive," said Dad. "At least Miss Gordon is giving you a second chance."

"I'm positive I don't want to take that quiz again," said Frankie.

"Would you rather fail math?" said Mom.

"I was thinking about it," said Frankie.

"If you do that," said Piper, "you'll be stuck in the same grade *forever.*"

"That's true," said Dad. "Before you know it, Lucy will catch up to you."

"She's already very good at subtraction," said Mom.

Frankie looked over at Lucy, who was sucking Cocoa Loops off of her placemat like a vacuum.

Could she really end up being his class-
mate?

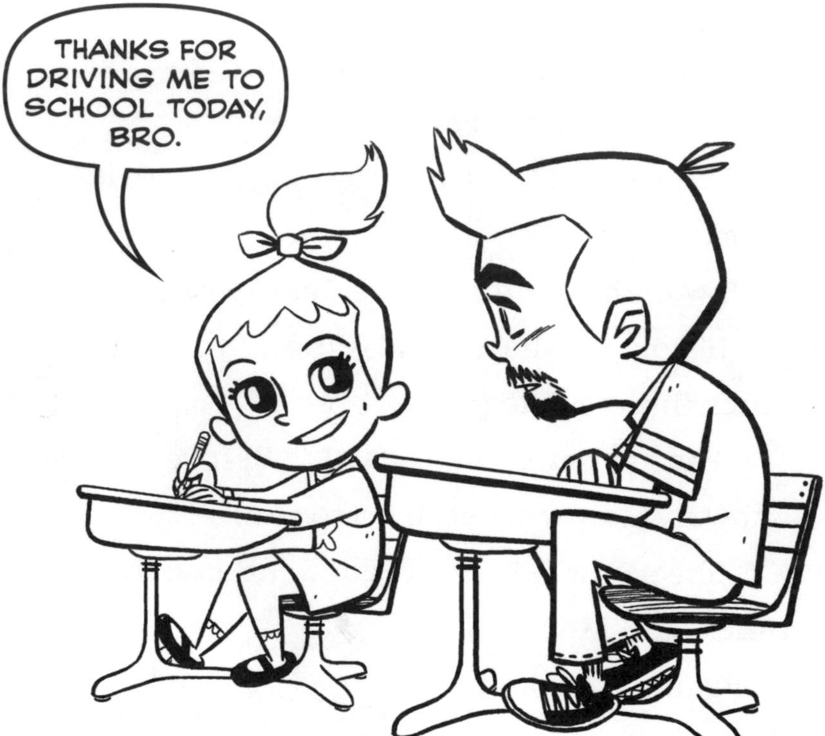
THANKS FOR DRIVING ME TO SCHOOL TODAY, BRO.

"That would be hilarious!" said Piper.

"Yeah, *hilarious*," said Frankie. He was anything but laughing.

CHAPTER SEVEN

An hour later there was a knock at Frankie's door.

"I brought baked goods," said Dad through Frankie's door.

"I'm not hungry," said Frankie, wiping the tears off his face with his pillowcase.

"You don't want dessert?" said Dad. He slowly entered Frankie's room and set a plate of cookies next to his bed. "This is way more serious than I thought."

"Everybody thinks I'm stupid," Frankie said with a sniffle.

"No one thinks that. We were just trying to show you how important it was to pass your quiz."

"Maybe it's not me. Maybe the world would be better off without math."

"How do you figure?" said Dad.

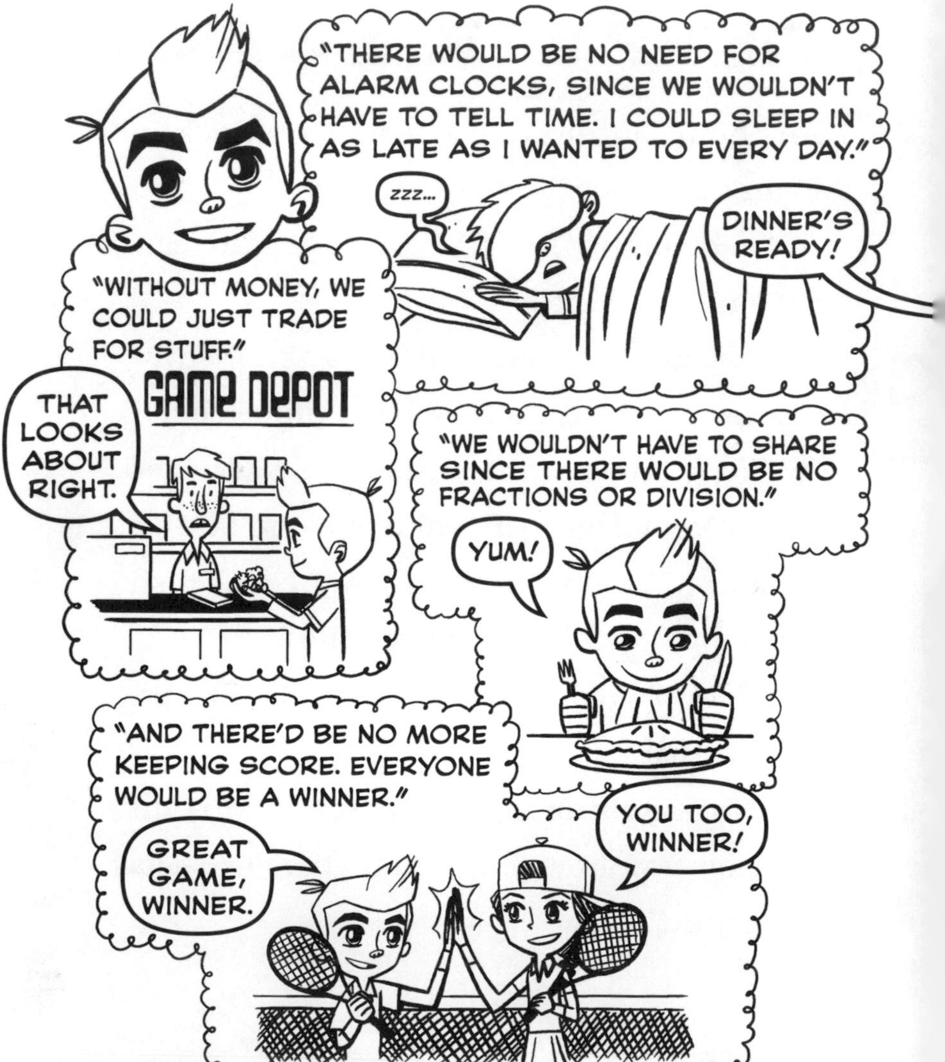
"THERE WOULD BE NO NEED FOR ALARM CLOCKS, SINCE WE WOULDN'T HAVE TO TELL TIME. I COULD SLEEP IN AS LATE AS I WANTED TO EVERY DAY."
ZZZ...
DINNER'S READY!
"WITHOUT MONEY, WE COULD JUST TRADE FOR STUFF."
GAME DEPOT
THAT LOOKS ABOUT RIGHT.
"WE WOULDN'T HAVE TO SHARE SINCE THERE WOULD BE NO FRACTIONS OR DIVISION."
YUM!
"AND THERE'D BE NO MORE KEEPING SCORE. EVERYONE WOULD BE A WINNER."
GREAT GAME, WINNER.
YOU TOO, WINNER!

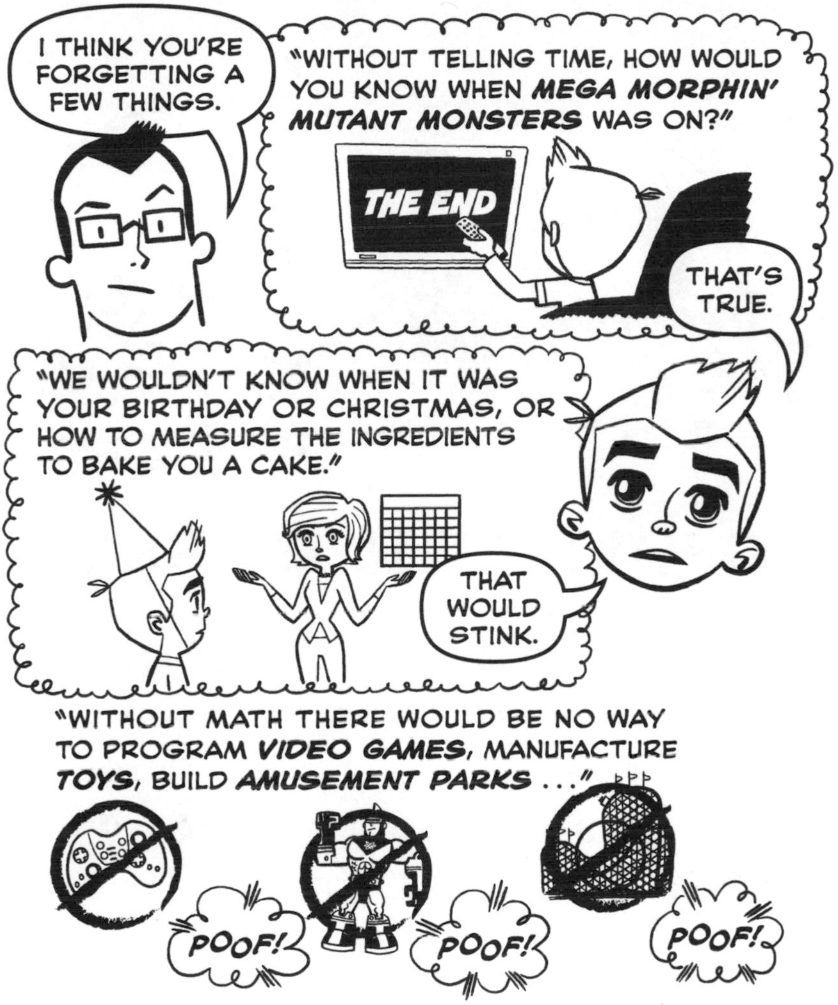
I THINK YOU'RE FORGETTING A FEW THINGS.
"WITHOUT TELLING TIME, HOW WOULD YOU KNOW WHEN *MEGA MORPHIN' MUTANT MONSTERS* WAS ON?"
THE END
THAT'S TRUE.
"WE WOULDN'T KNOW WHEN IT WAS YOUR BIRTHDAY OR CHRISTMAS, OR HOW TO MEASURE THE INGREDIENTS TO BAKE YOU A CAKE."
THAT WOULD STINK.
"WITHOUT MATH THERE WOULD BE NO WAY TO PROGRAM *VIDEO GAMES*, MANUFACTURE *TOYS*, BUILD *AMUSEMENT PARKS* . . ."
POOF!
POOF!
POOF!

"Okay, I get it," said Frankie. "You need math for everything." He buried his head under his pillow. "I'm so doomed."

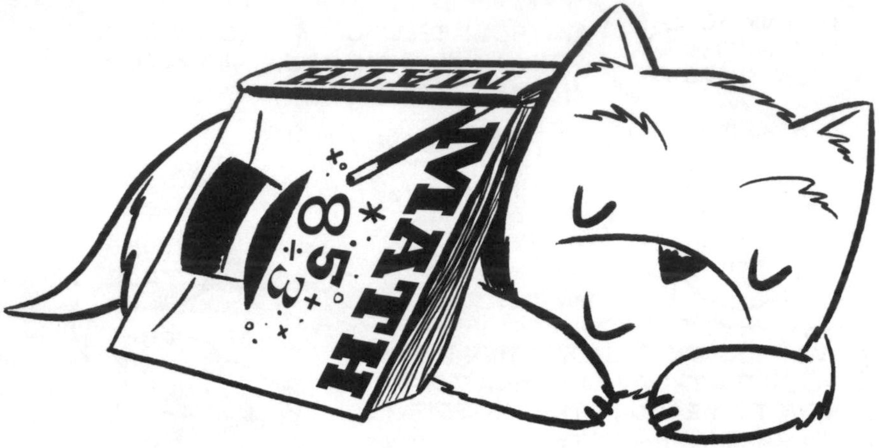
MATH
MATH
8 * 5 ÷ 3 +

CHAPTER EIGHT

"It's nothing a little extra studying can't solve," said Dad as he left Frankie's room. Frankie wasn't so convinced. Argyle curled up next to him, more interested in snuggling than schoolwork.

"Dogs are so lucky," said Frankie. "You don't need to know math." But then he remembered that dogs also can't play video games or eat chocolate, so maybe they weren't so lucky after all.

Maybe Dad was right. Frankie decided to give studying a try. Nibbling on a peanut butter–marshmallow cookie, he cracked open his textbook. Page after page of numbers and squiggles. The more he stared at it, the more it turned his brain into goo. How was he ever going to remember this stuff? He would fail his math quiz again for sure!

Frustrated, he hurled his textbook across the room, knocking over a shelf of tin robots. Argyle scurried for cover under Frankie's bed.

Mom poked her head into his room. "Everything okay in here?"

"I was practicing division," Frankie said with a huff.

Mom looked over at the wreckage on the floor. "You're lucky you didn't end up with fractions."

Frankie turned the color of a tomato. "I hate math! I'm never going to pass my quiz! I'm going to be stuck in the same grade *FOREVER*!!"

Mom put her arm around Frankie to calm him. "I think you've had enough math for today," she said. "Everything will seem a little less impossible after a good night's sleep."

Frankie couldn't get into his pajamas and under the covers fast enough. He might not be able to avoid math forever, but at least he was done with it for tonight. He didn't even need to count sheep to fall asleep.

CHAPTER NINE

"Rise and shine, Rip van Pickle."

Frankie cracked open one eye. Mom was going through his closet, coordinating an outfit for him to wear.

"What's with the clothes?" said Frankie.

"Dad and Piper are at field hockey practice, so you'll have to come with Lucy and me to the supermarket."

"But what about my quiz?"

"Don't worry, there will be plenty of time to study when we get back."

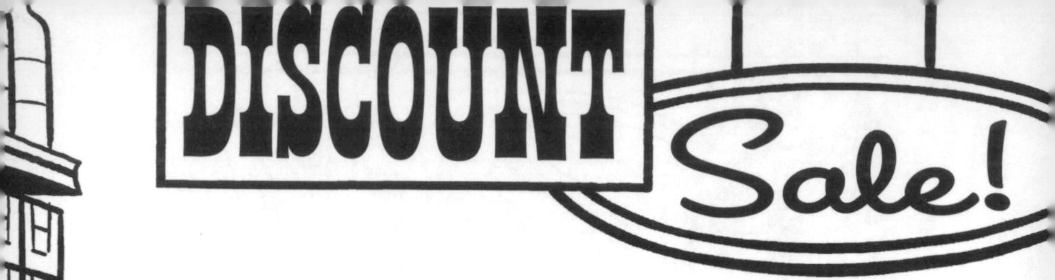
DISCOUNT
Sale!

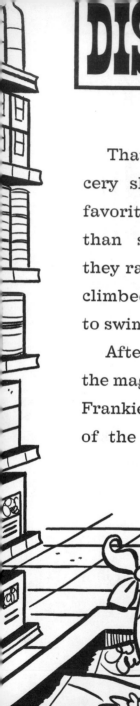

That's what Frankie was afraid of. Grocery shopping wasn't exactly Frankie's favorite activity, but it was way better than studying math. Especially when they raced shopping carts, or when Lucy climbed into the frozen food bin and tried to swim in it like it was a ball pit.

After Lucy thawed out, they passed the magazine aisle. Something caught Frankie's eye. It was the latest issue of the *Awesome Adventures of*

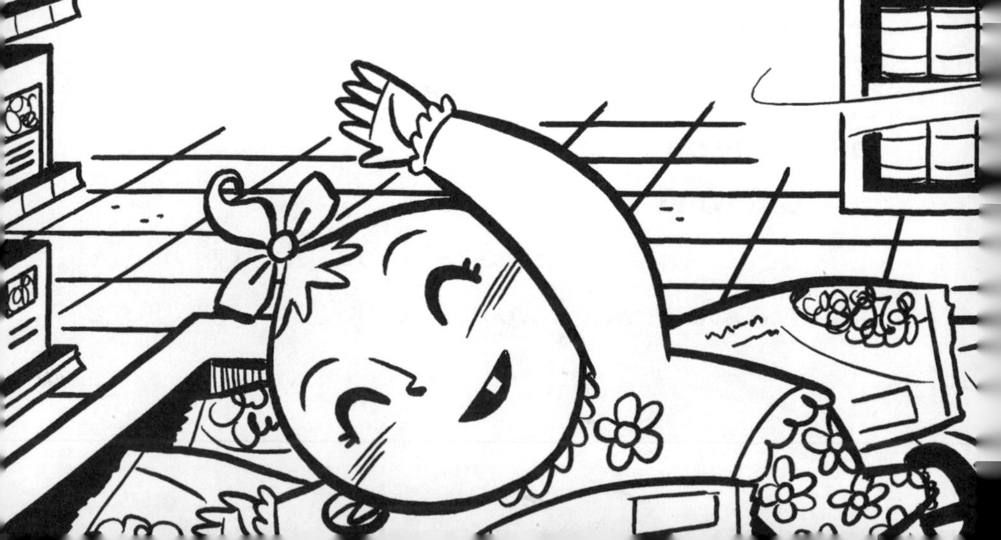

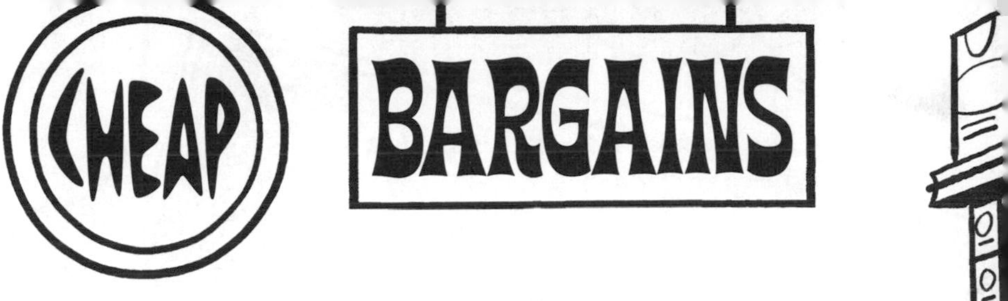
CHEAP
BARGAINS

Captain Atomic! Who knew what heroic hijinks waited for Frankie inside that shrink-wrapped packaging?

He hugged the comic book over his heart. "Mom, pleeease can I get this? Please, please, pretty please, please?"

"Sorry, Frankie, but I only brought enough money to pay for the groceries on this list. Maybe next time."

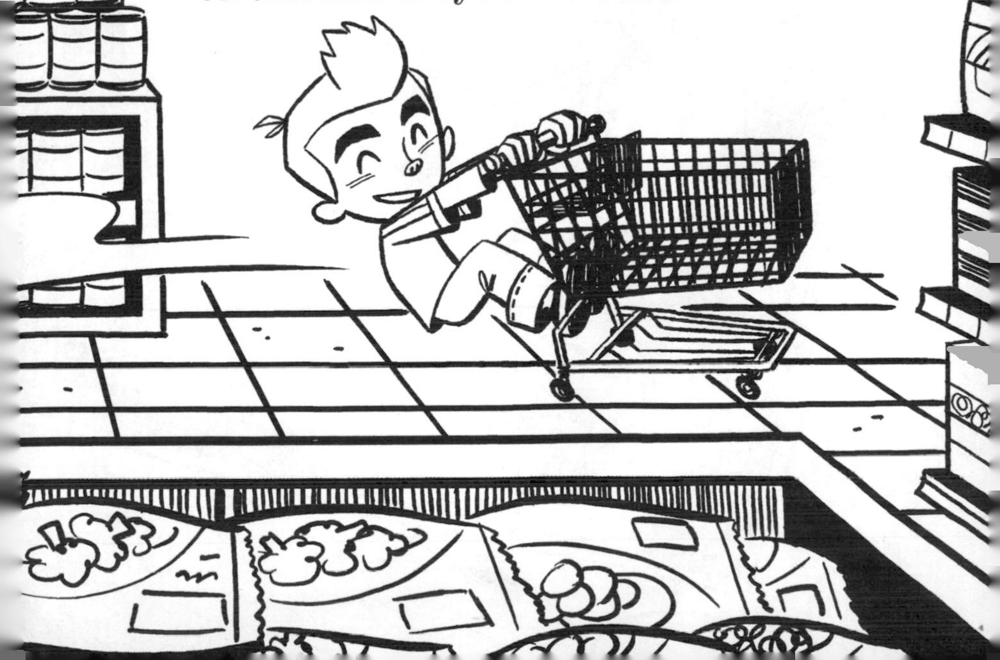

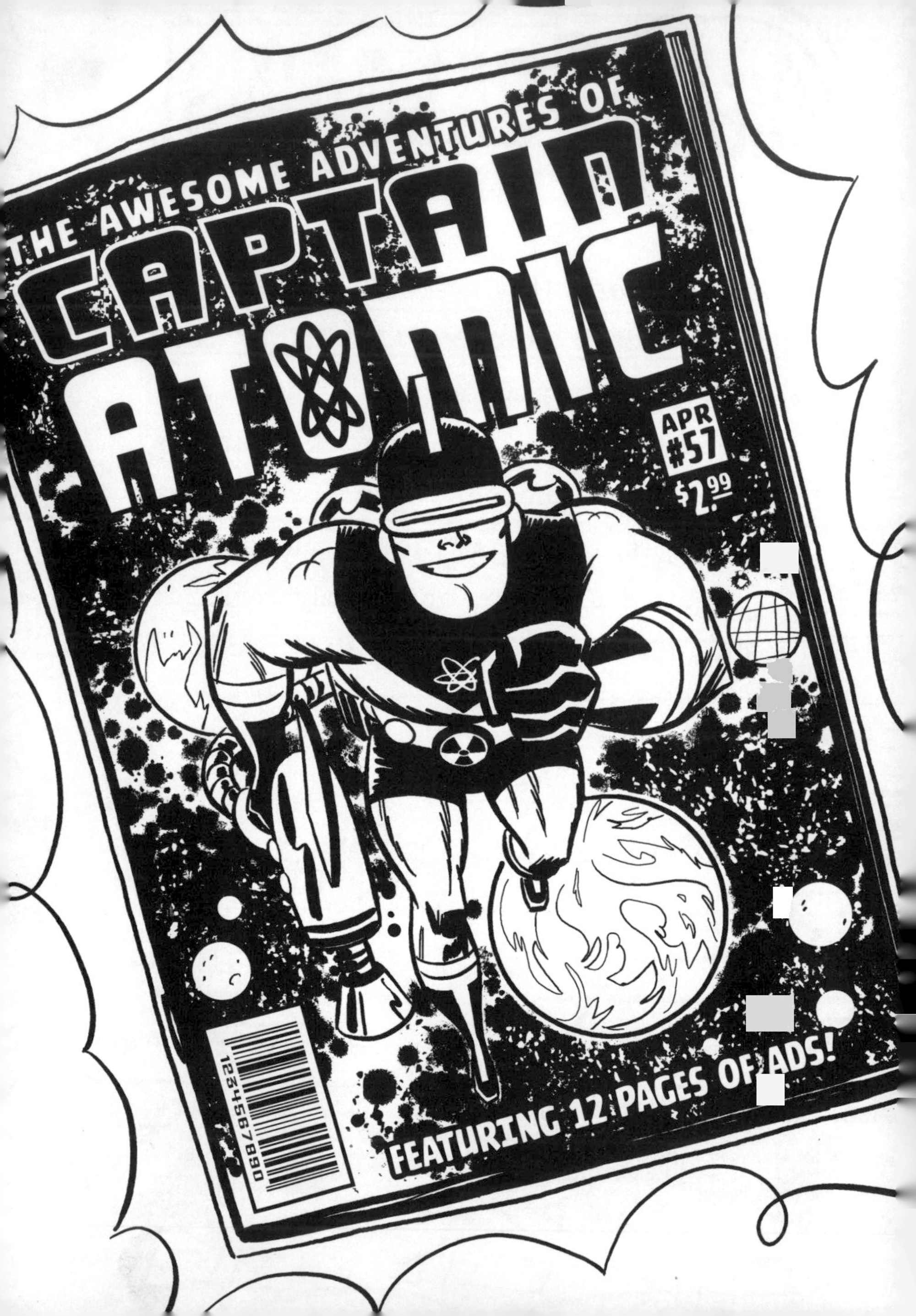
THE AWESOME ADVENTURES OF
CAPTAIN ATOMIC
APR #57
$2.99
FEATURING 12 PAGES OF ADS!

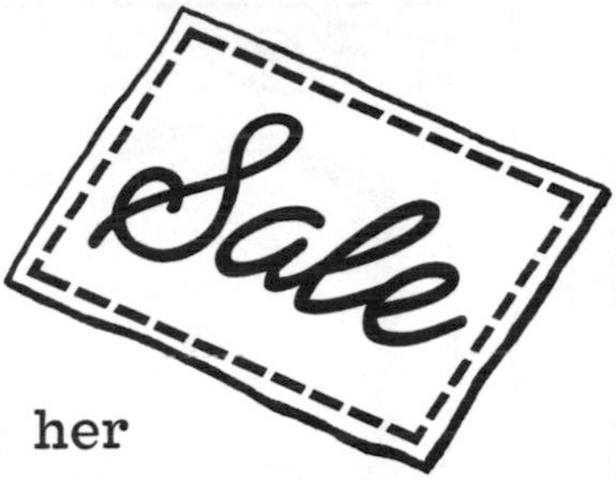
Sale

"But it's the last copy! We could put back some vegetables."

Before Mom could begin her lecture on the importance of roughage, she was interrupted by the broadcast of a store-wide announcement. "Attention ShopMart shoppers, we have a special on turkey jerky: buy 2 get 1 half price."

Frankie looked at the tag on the shelf. "That'll save us $.25."

"Tell you what," said Mom. "I bet there are other coupons and sales around the store. If you can save us enough money to pay for your comic book, you can get it."

"It's a deal!" said Frankie.

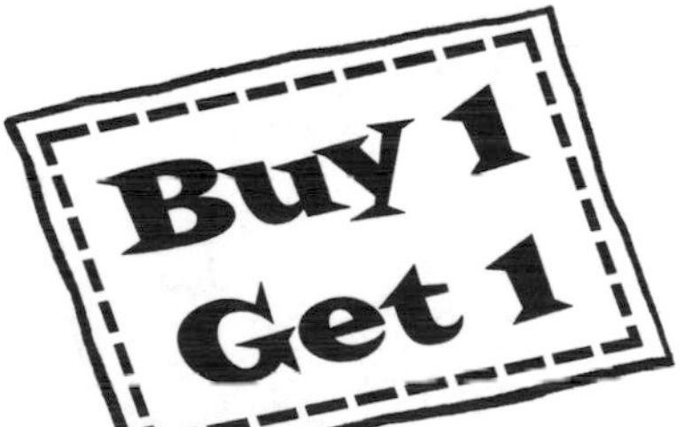
Buy 1
Get 1

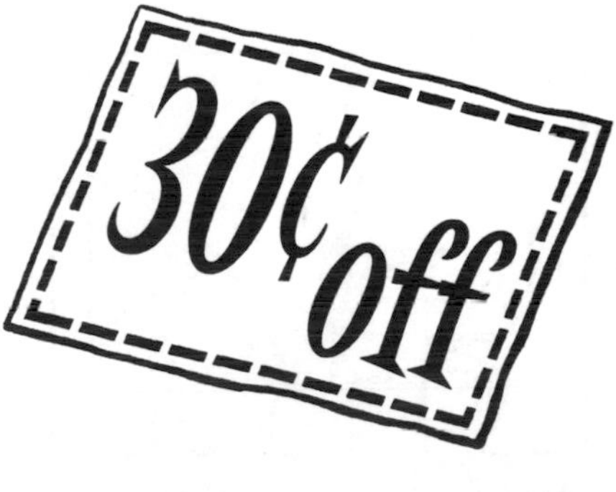
30¢ off

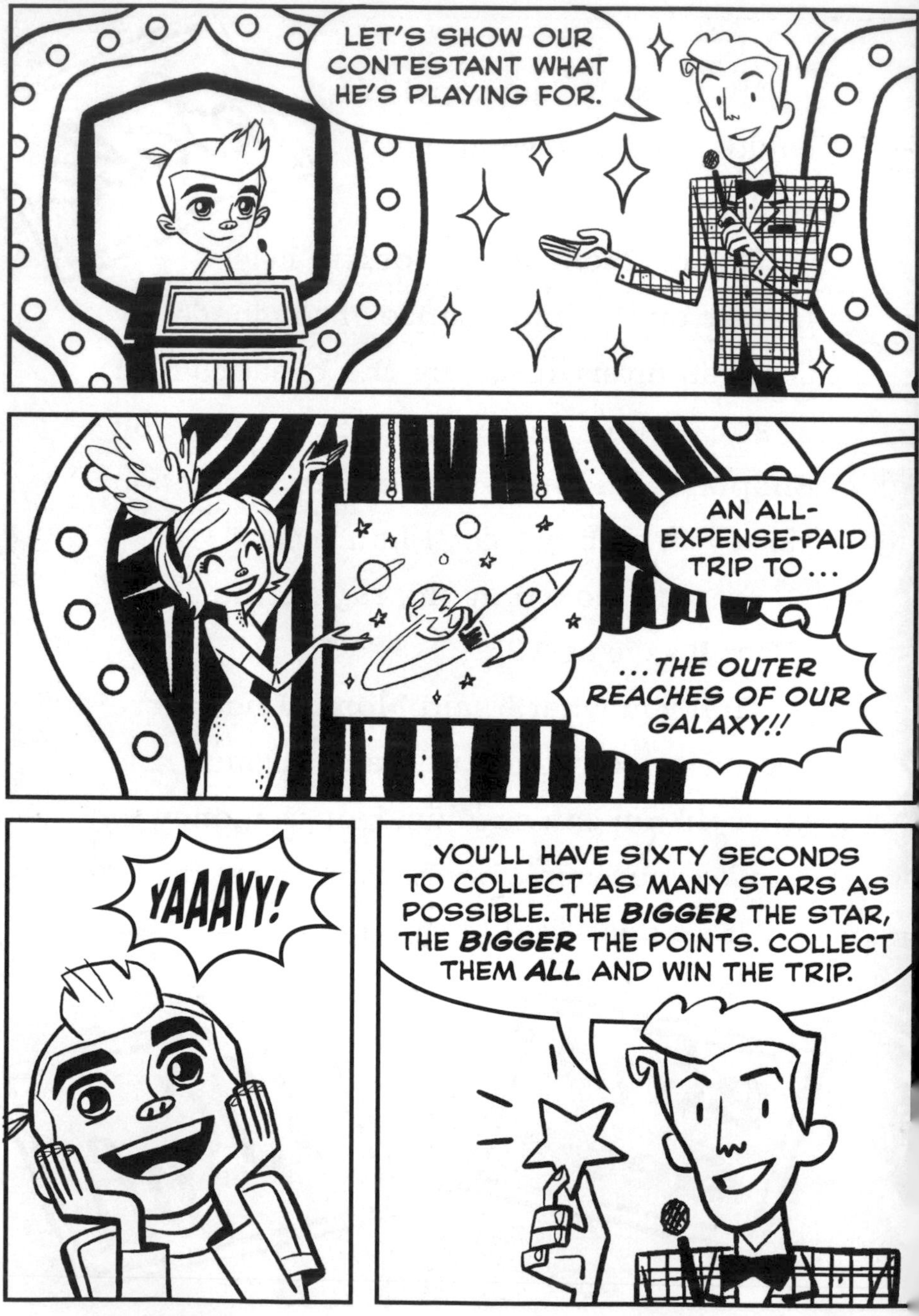
LET'S SHOW OUR CONTESTANT WHAT HE'S PLAYING FOR.
AN ALL-EXPENSE-PAID TRIP TO...
...THE OUTER REACHES OF OUR GALAXY!!
YAAAYY!
YOU'LL HAVE SIXTY SECONDS TO COLLECT AS MANY STARS AS POSSIBLE. THE BIGGER THE STAR, THE BIGGER THE POINTS. COLLECT THEM ALL AND WIN THE TRIP.

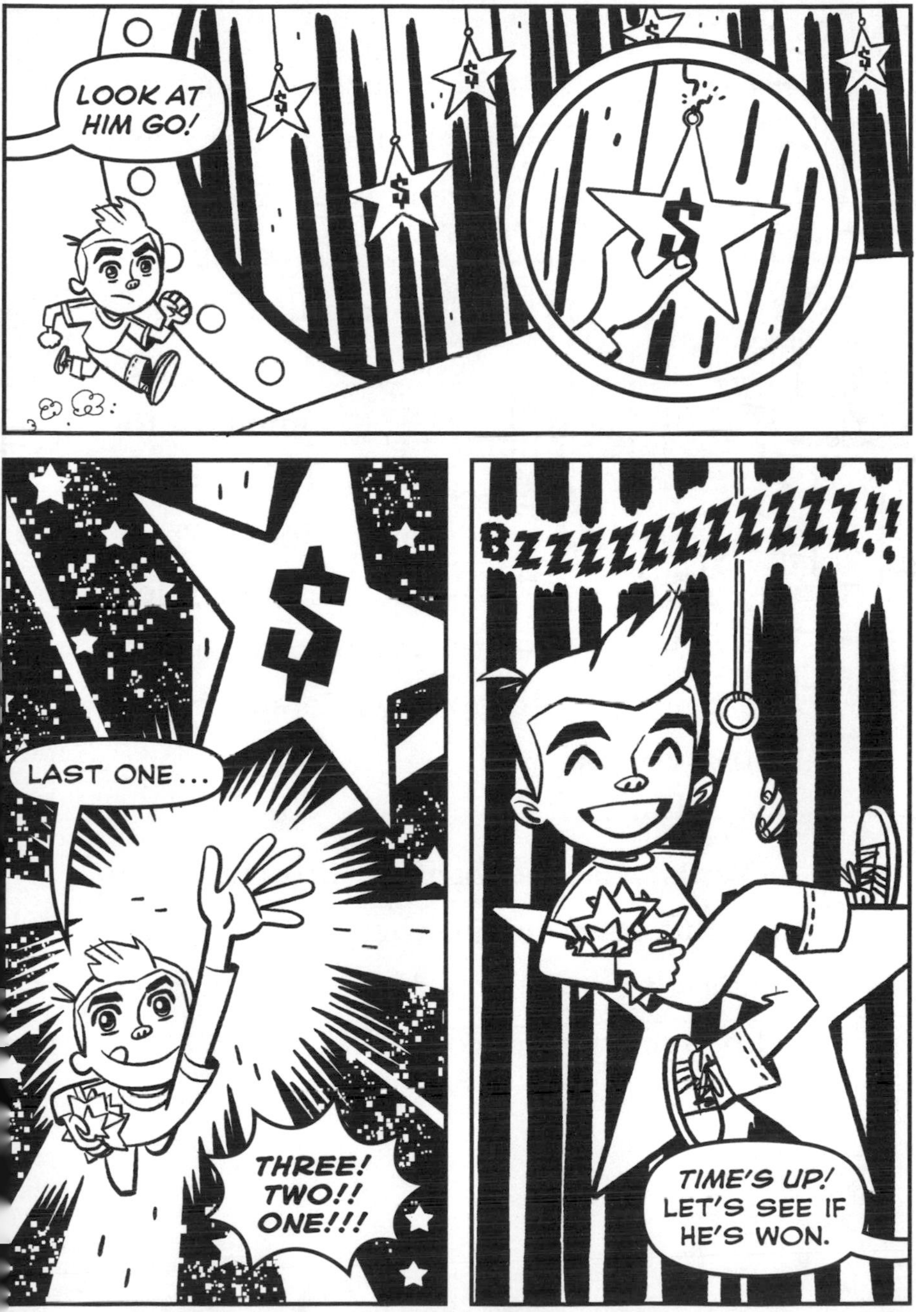
LOOK AT HIM GO!
LAST ONE...
THREE! TWO!! ONE!!!
BZZZZZZZZZZZZZ!!
TIME'S UP! LET'S SEE IF HE'S WON.

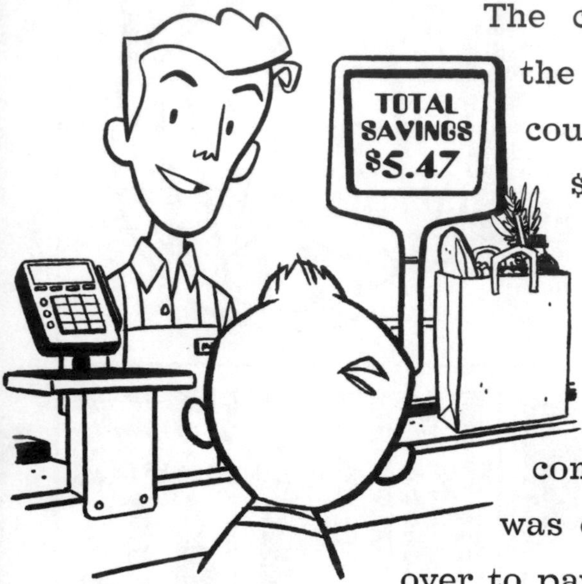
TOTAL
SAVINGS
$5.47

The cashier scanned the last of Frankie's coupons. "You saved $5.47 today," he said.

More than enough for Frankie's comic book! There was even money left over to pay for the bag of peas Lucy gnawed open while she was in the freezer bin.

Ka-ching!

Frankie dashed back to the magazine aisle. But when he got there, the Captain Atomic comic book was gone. Someone else had bought the last copy!

CHAPTER TEN

What a bummer. All that hard work, and Frankie couldn't even claim his prize. Mom pinkie swore that she would find the new Captain Atomic comic book as soon as she could. But for now, they had to get home or else the groceries would spoil.

The day was half over already, which meant Frankie had better get some studying done. As soon as he finished helping Mom unpack the groceries, he was heading straight to his room to do exactly that.

Or that was the plan, at least.

There was a knock at the front door.

Actually, it was *knock, knock-knock, tap-tap-tap, knock, knock, tap*. Only one person other than Frankie knew this super-secret code: his best friend, Kenny.

"Hey, Kenny. I don't think I can hang out today. I have to study for my ma—"

Kenny held out a zipper-top bag filled with Yugimon cards. Frankie was helpless against the power of Yugimon.

They raced upstairs to do battle. Sitting across from each other on Frankie's floor, Kenny held up a small stack of Yugimon cards, like he was about to demonstrate

a magic trick, and arranged 12 cards in a
grid pattern.

Frankie was confused. "That's not how
you play Yugimon."

Ignoring him, Kenny took a small flute
out of his shirt pocket and blew out two
notes. Then he divided the cards into two
equal piles.

"I get it—2 notes, 2 groups," said Frankie.

Kenny shuffled all of the cards back together and handed them to Frankie. Then he played 3 notes with the flute and pointed to Frankie.

"You want me to do the dividing part?" said Frankie. Kenny nodded. Frankie made 3 piles, each having 4 cards.

"That the best you can do?" said Frankie.

Kenny smiled, then reached into his

pocket and pulled out another sandwich bag filled with Yugimon cards. He added them to the pile.

"Bring it on," said Frankie.

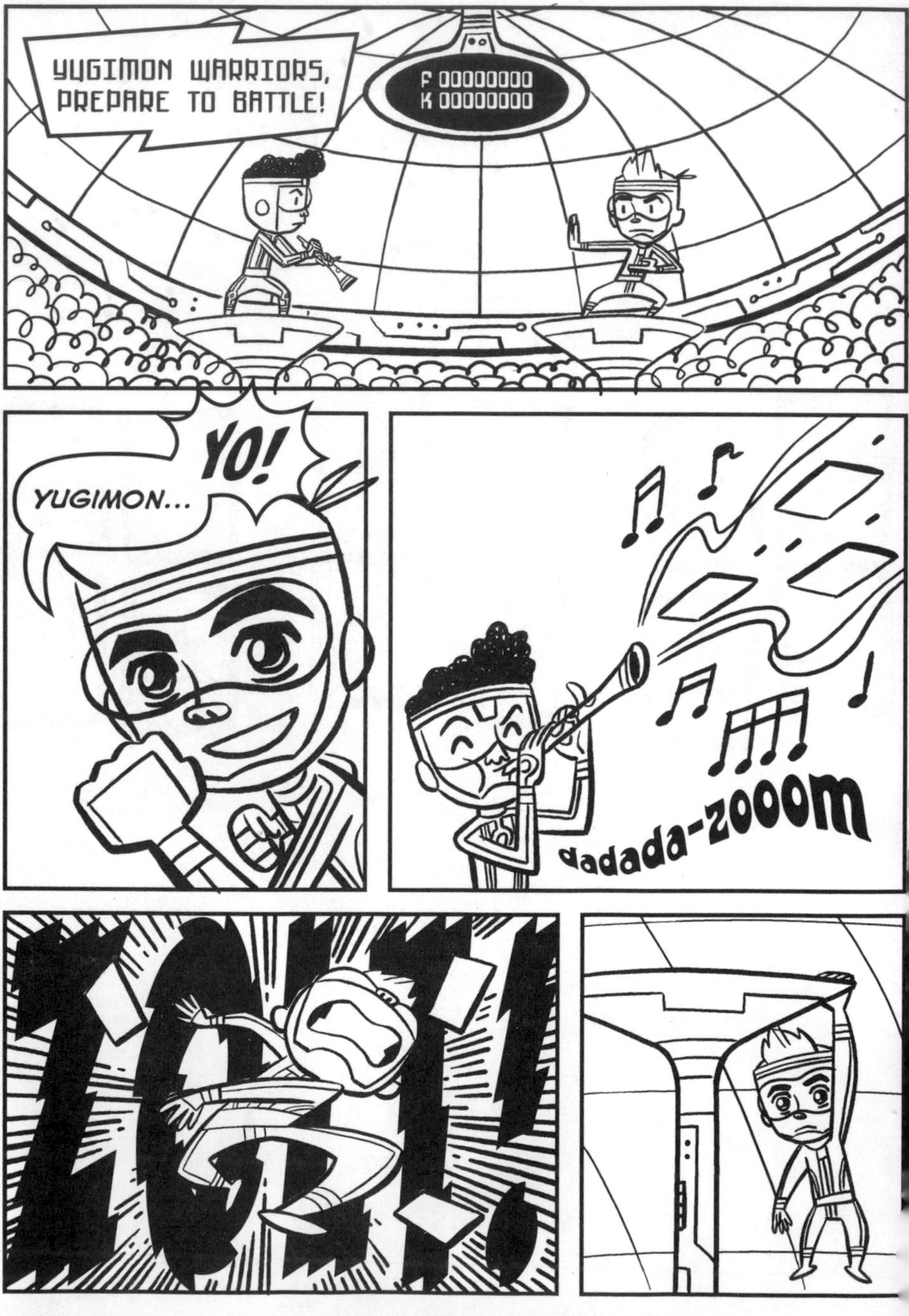
YUGIMON WARRIORS, PREPARE TO BATTLE!
F 00000000
K 00000000
YUGIMON... YO!
dadada-ZOOOM

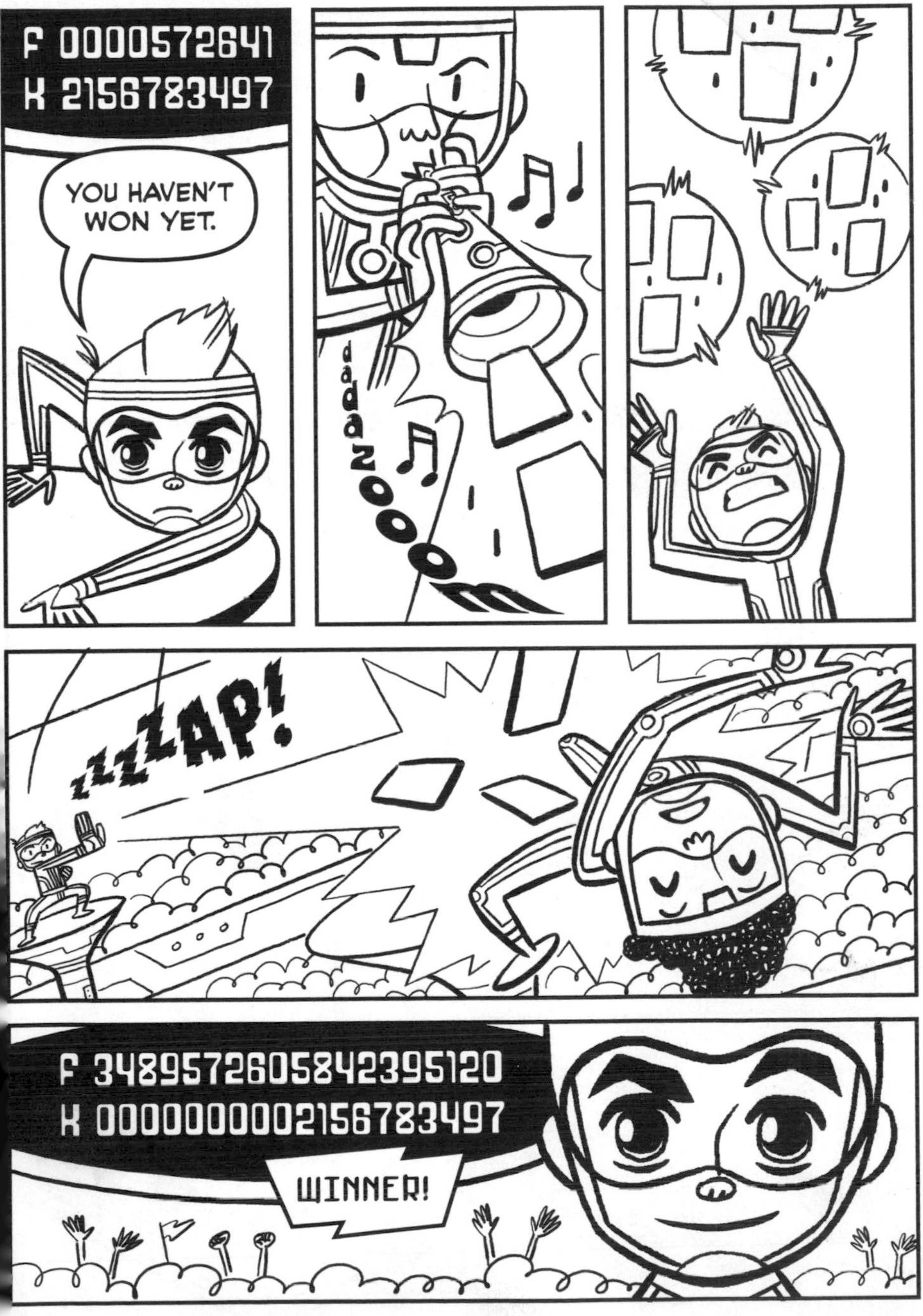
F 0000572641
K 2156783497
YOU HAVEN'T WON YET.
zzzZAP!
F 348957260584239512O
K 00000000002156783497
WINNER!

Frankie was having such a blast playing Yugimon with Kenny, he had no idea of how late it had gotten until Mom called them down to dinner.

After they had eaten and Kenny had gone home, Frankie kept telling himself that he needed to study. But there was a new episode of *Mega Morphin' Mutant Monsters* on TV, and then it was bath time, and by then Frankie was too tired to even think about math.

It would have to wait until tomorrow.

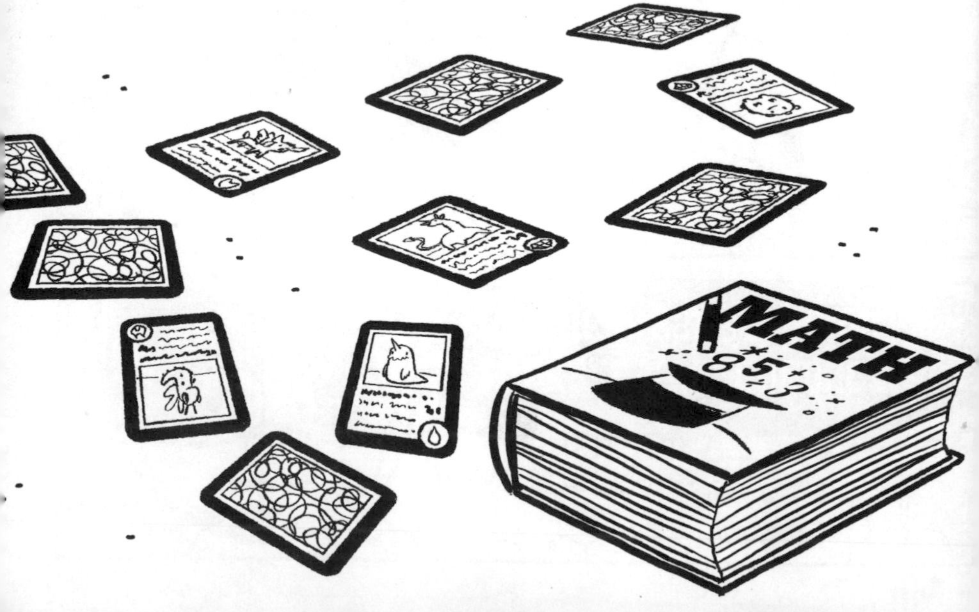
MATH
85
3

CHAPTER ELEVEN

Frankie wrapped himself in blankets, trying to avoid the morning sun like a vampire. But then he thought about his math quiz. Time was running out, and if he didn't start studying, he would fail his quiz again for sure. Maybe what he needed was a change of scenery.

Frankie fetched his textbook and headed for the backyard. Unfortunately, someone else was already there.

Piper had transformed the backyard into her personal exercise facility, or as she liked to call it, her Playground of Pain.

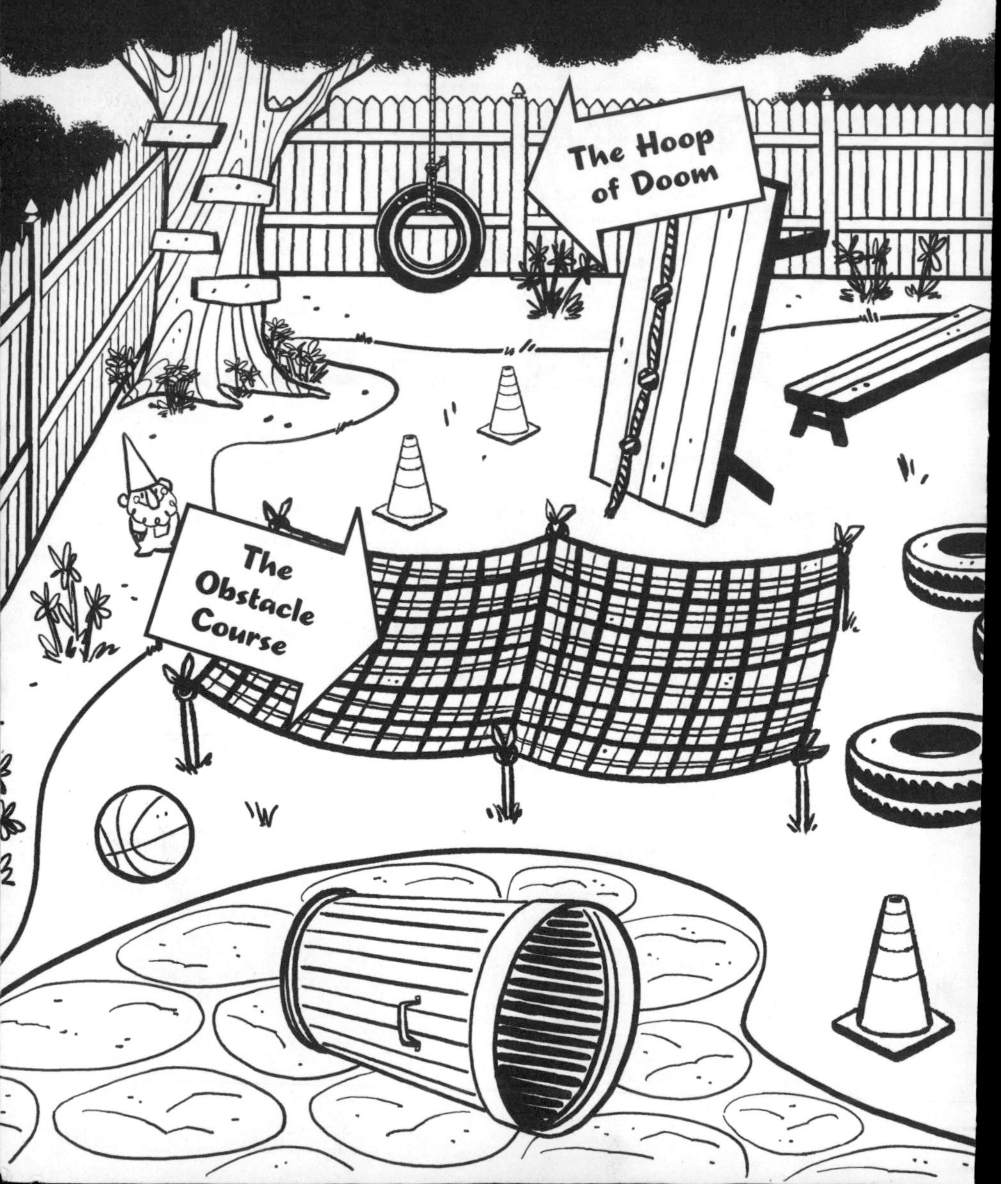

The Hoop of Doom
The Obstacle Course

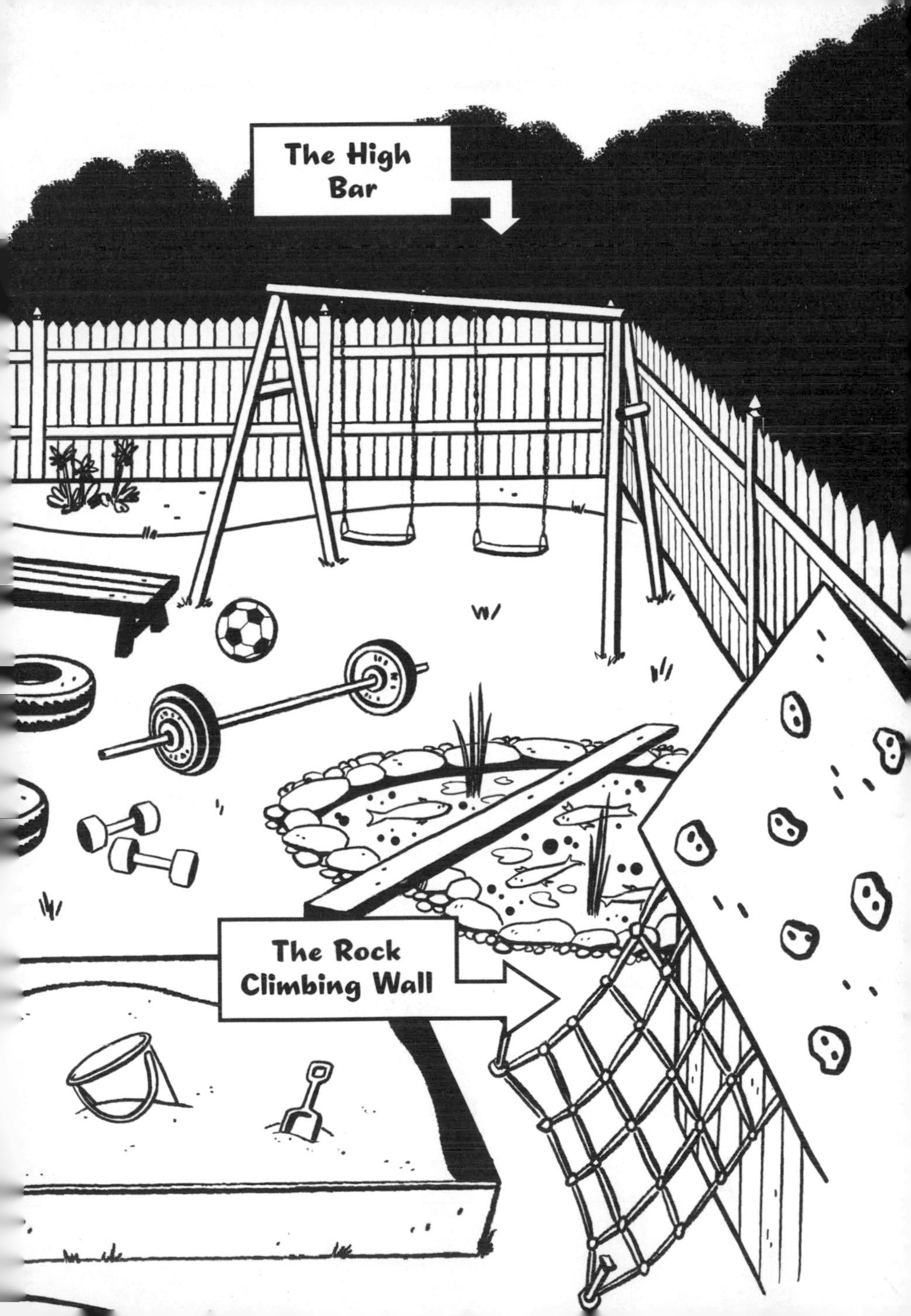
The High Bar
The Rock Climbing Wall

Frankie watched as Piper did chin-ups on the swing set. He lost count of how many she had completed, and she was still going strong. There was no way Frankie would be able to concentrate with all of her huffing and puffing while she exercised. He turned to go back inside.

"Where are you going?" said Piper between grunts.

"I need to find somewhere quiet to study for my math quiz," said Frankie.

"I've got a better idea," said Piper. She dropped to the ground and fetched a football out of a plastic bin filled with sports equipment. "Want to play catch?"

Frankie was so shocked,

he looked over his shoulder to make sure she wasn't talking to someone else. "But you *never* want to play catch with me."

Piper smiled. "Then you better go long before I change my mind."

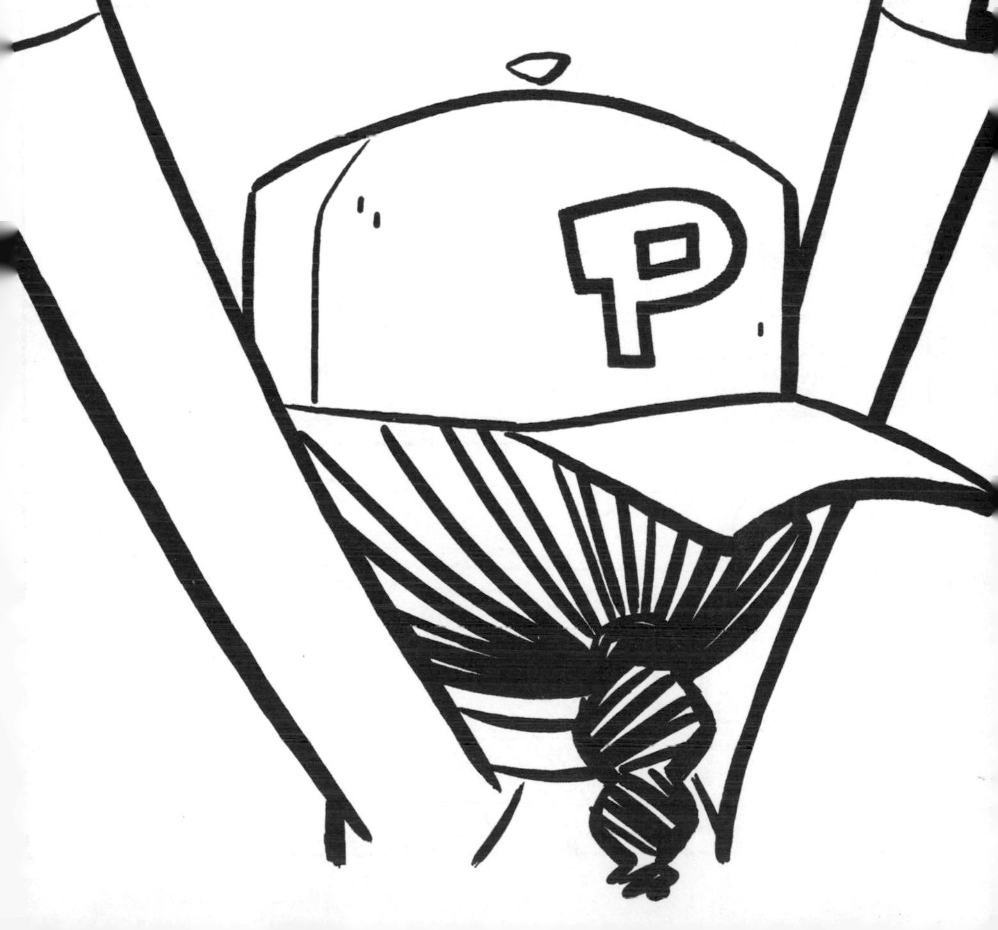

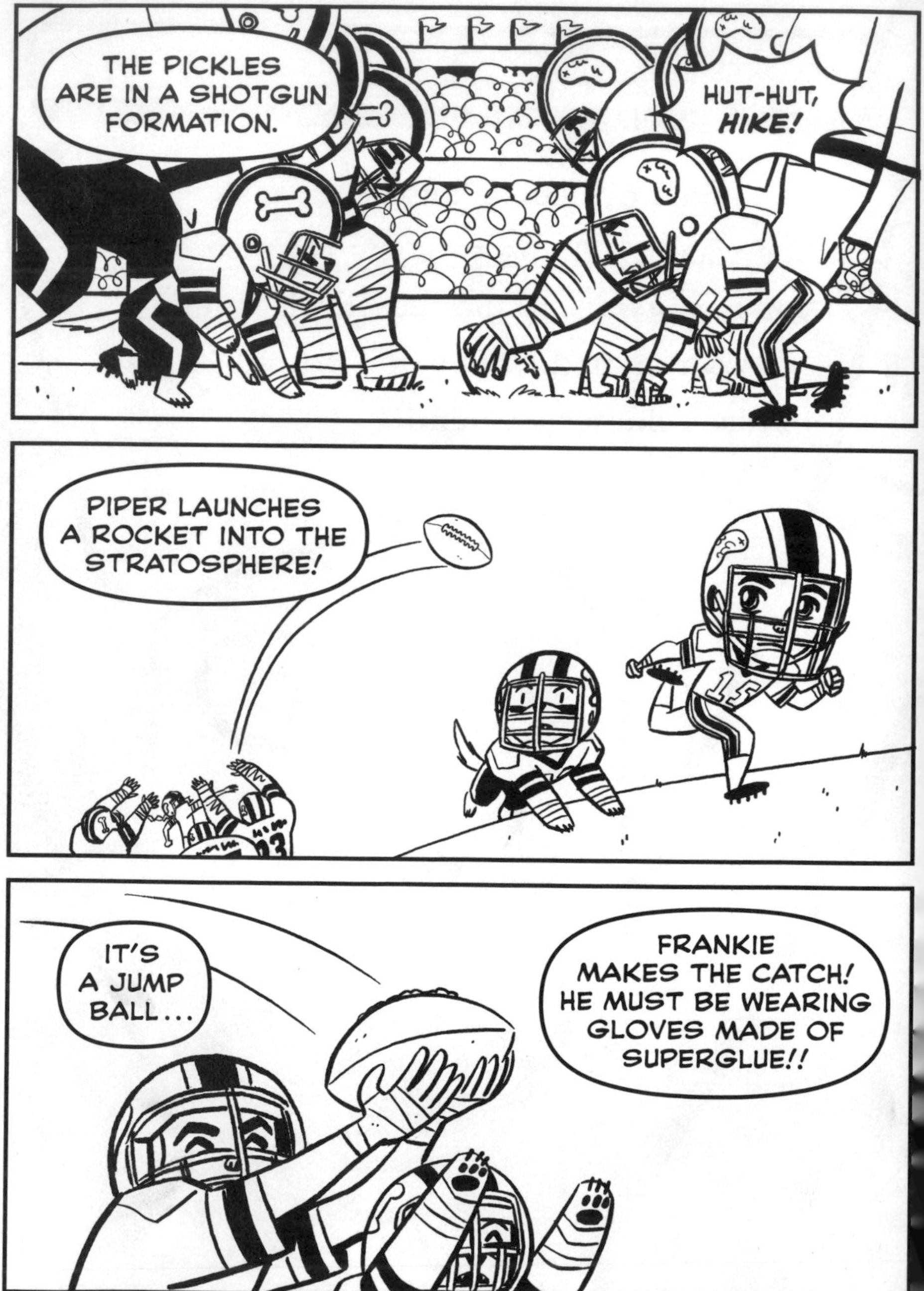
THE PICKLES ARE IN A SHOTGUN FORMATION.
HUT-HUT, *HIKE!*
PIPER LAUNCHES A ROCKET INTO THE STRATOSPHERE!
IT'S A JUMP BALL...
FRANKIE MAKES THE CATCH! HE MUST BE WEARING GLOVES MADE OF SUPERGLUE!!

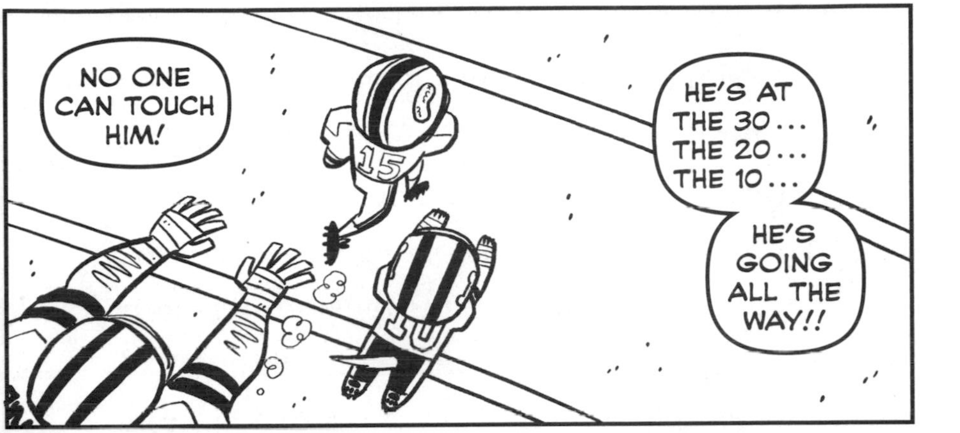
NO ONE CAN TOUCH HIM!
HE'S AT THE 30... THE 20... THE 10...
HE'S GOING ALL THE WAY!!

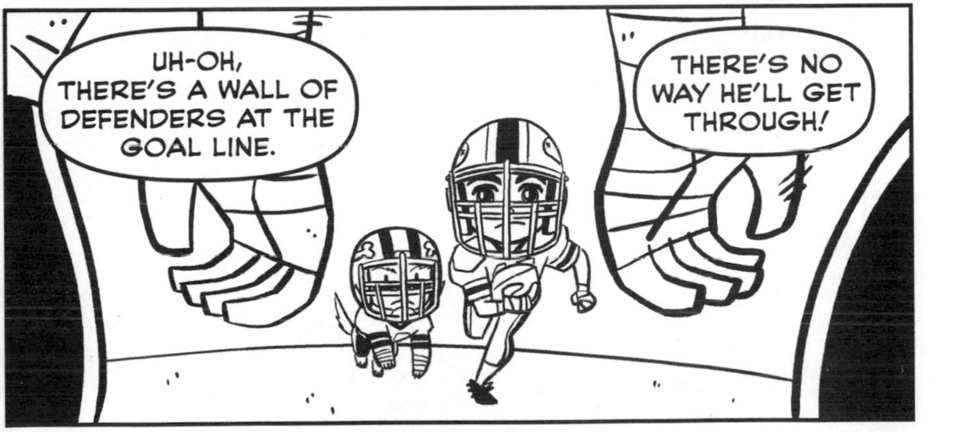
UH-OH, THERE'S A WALL OF DEFENDERS AT THE GOAL LINE.
THERE'S NO WAY HE'LL GET THROUGH!

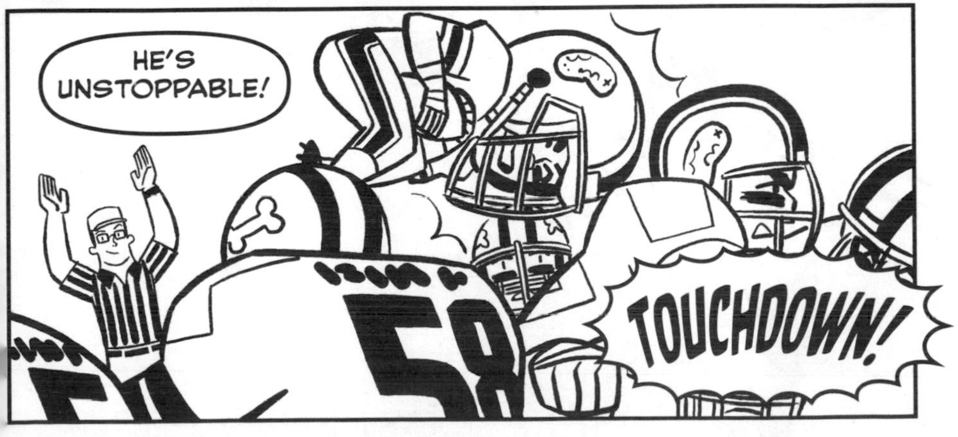
HE'S UNSTOPPABLE!
TOUCHDOWN!

Frankie and Piper gave each other a leaping high five. Without stopping to catch his breath, Frankie was off again, running, catching, scoring. They did this again and again until his legs felt like jelly.

"How many was that?" said Piper.

Frankie wiped the sweat off his face with his T-shirt. "6. Would have been 7, but that flower pot came out of nowhere."

"So if each is worth 6 points, what's the score?"

"Hmm . . . 6 + 6 + 6 + 6 + 6 + 6 = 36."

"Not bad," said Piper, spinning the football on her finger like a top. "Bet I can beat it."

CHAPTER TWELVE

"What happened to you?" said Dad.

"Piper," said Frankie as he limped into the kitchen. His hair was bent in odd directions, and his clothes were covered with grass stains. "I was trying to study math."

"You look like she beat it into you," said Dad. He was arranging ingredients on the kitchen counter. When it came to baking, Dad was a wizard in the kitchen. Recipes were his spells, his wooden spoon a magic wand.

"Whatcha making?" said Frankie.

"I'm testing out a new chocolate-zucchini muffin recipe," said Dad.

"Sounds healthy."

"Want to give me a hand?"

"For real?" Frankie needed to study, but he *loved* being Dad's apprentice. It meant he got to do fun stuff, like crack eggs, get messy with flour, and lick the spatula.

"As long as you wash up first," said Dad.

Studying would have to wait. Frankie bolted upstairs, returning a minute later, freshly scrubbed from head to toe. He even put on clean underwear. This was serious business.

Dad tied an apron around Frankie's waist, then handed him a whisk. They were ready to conjure up something delicious.

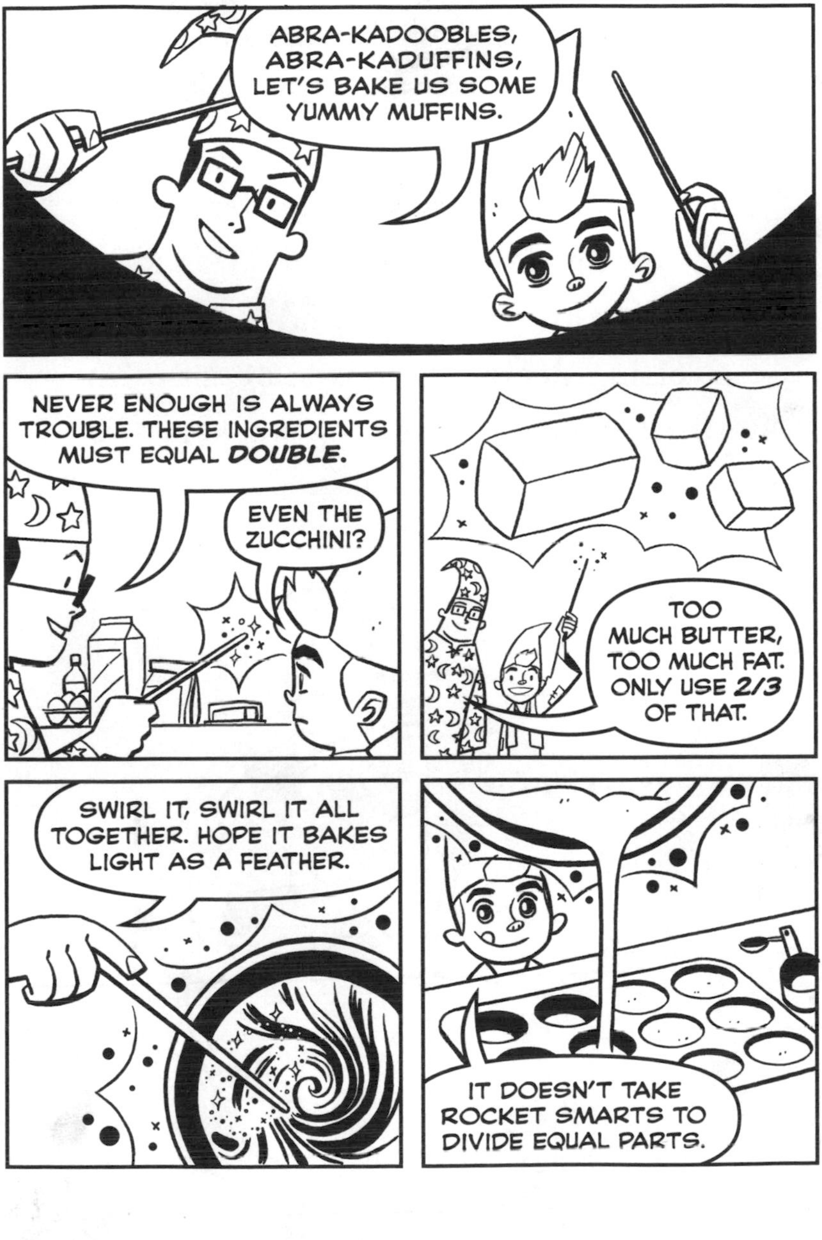
ABRA-KADOOBLES, ABRA-KADUFFINS, LET'S BAKE US SOME YUMMY MUFFINS.
NEVER ENOUGH IS ALWAYS TROUBLE. THESE INGREDIENTS MUST EQUAL ***DOUBLE***.
EVEN THE ZUCCHINI?
TOO MUCH BUTTER, TOO MUCH FAT. ONLY USE ***2/3*** OF THAT.
SWIRL IT, SWIRL IT ALL TOGETHER. HOPE IT BAKES LIGHT AS A FEATHER.
IT DOESN'T TAKE ROCKET SMARTS TO DIVIDE EQUAL PARTS.

Twenty-four-and-a-half minutes later, the chocolate-zucchini muffins were out of the oven and inside their bellies. Frankie even got to have an extra one after dinner for eating his lima beans.

Between all of the food and fun, Frankie was getting sleepy. He looked outside. The sun had begun to set. The weekend was almost over.

Wait a sec.

THE WEEKEND *WAS* ALMOST OVER!

SUNDAY
MONDAY
TUESDAY
WEDNESDAY
THURSDAY
FRIDAY
SATURDAY

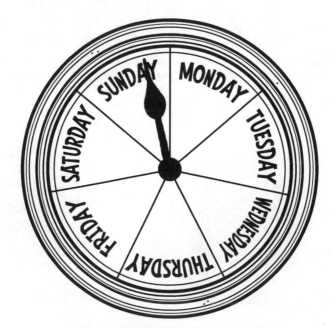

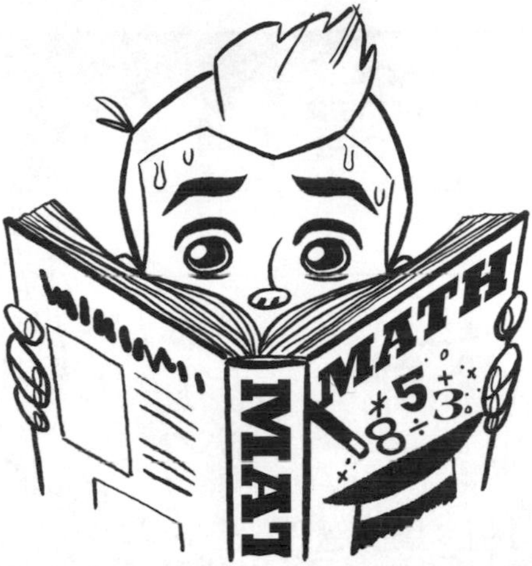
MATH
MAT

CHAPTER THIRTEEN

Two days had come and gone in a blink, and Frankie had barely studied for his math quiz. How could this have happened?!

He charged up to his bedroom. At best, he'd have an hour before Mom made him turn off his light. He threw open his textbook. So much to study. How was he ever going to cram all that he needed to learn into such a short amount of time?

He had to try. But the more he studied, the heavier his eyes became.

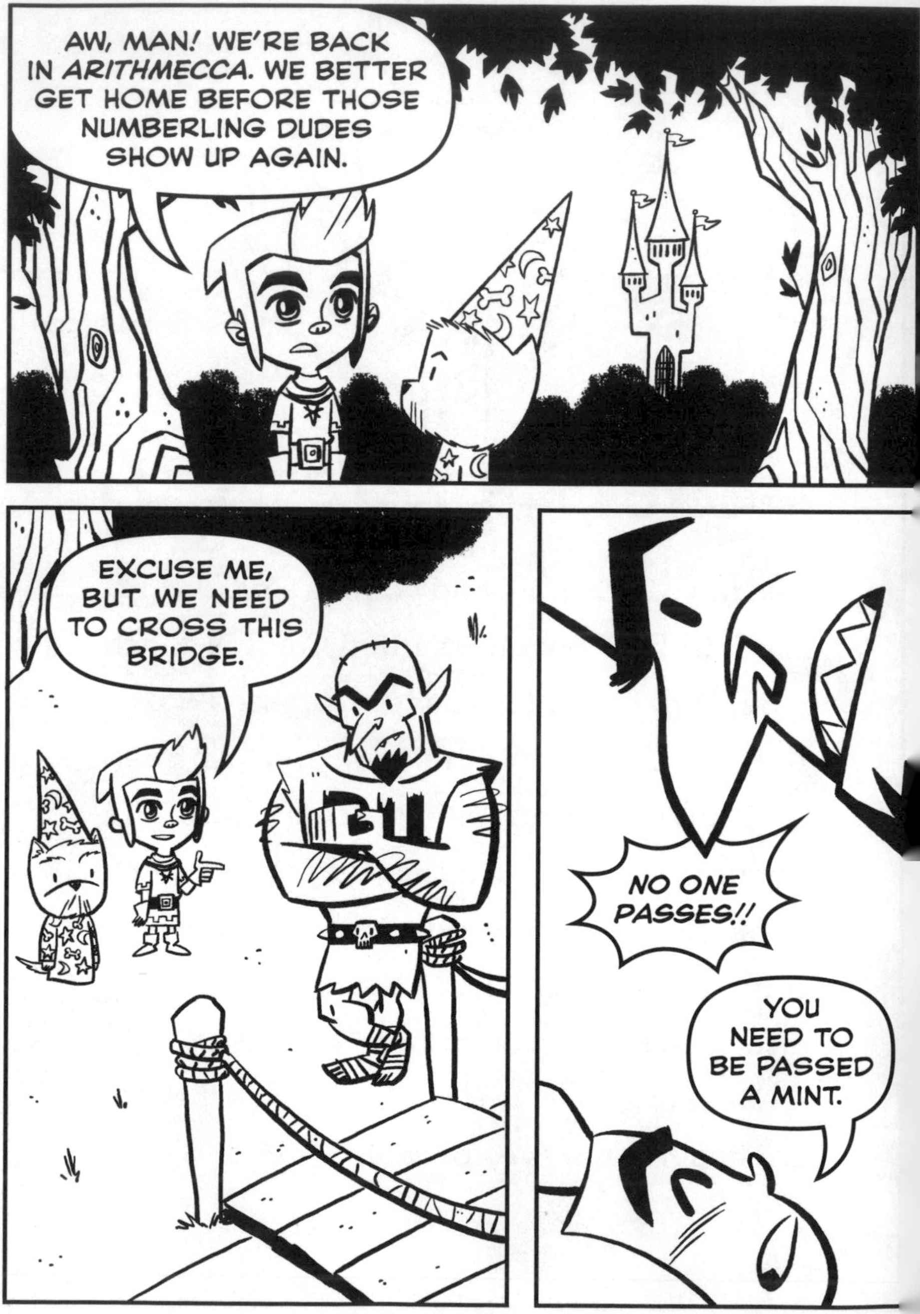
AW, MAN! WE'RE BACK IN *ARITHMECCA*. WE BETTER GET HOME BEFORE THOSE NUMBERLING DUDES SHOW UP AGAIN.
EXCUSE ME, BUT WE NEED TO CROSS THIS BRIDGE.
NO ONE PASSES!!
YOU NEED TO BE PASSED A MINT.

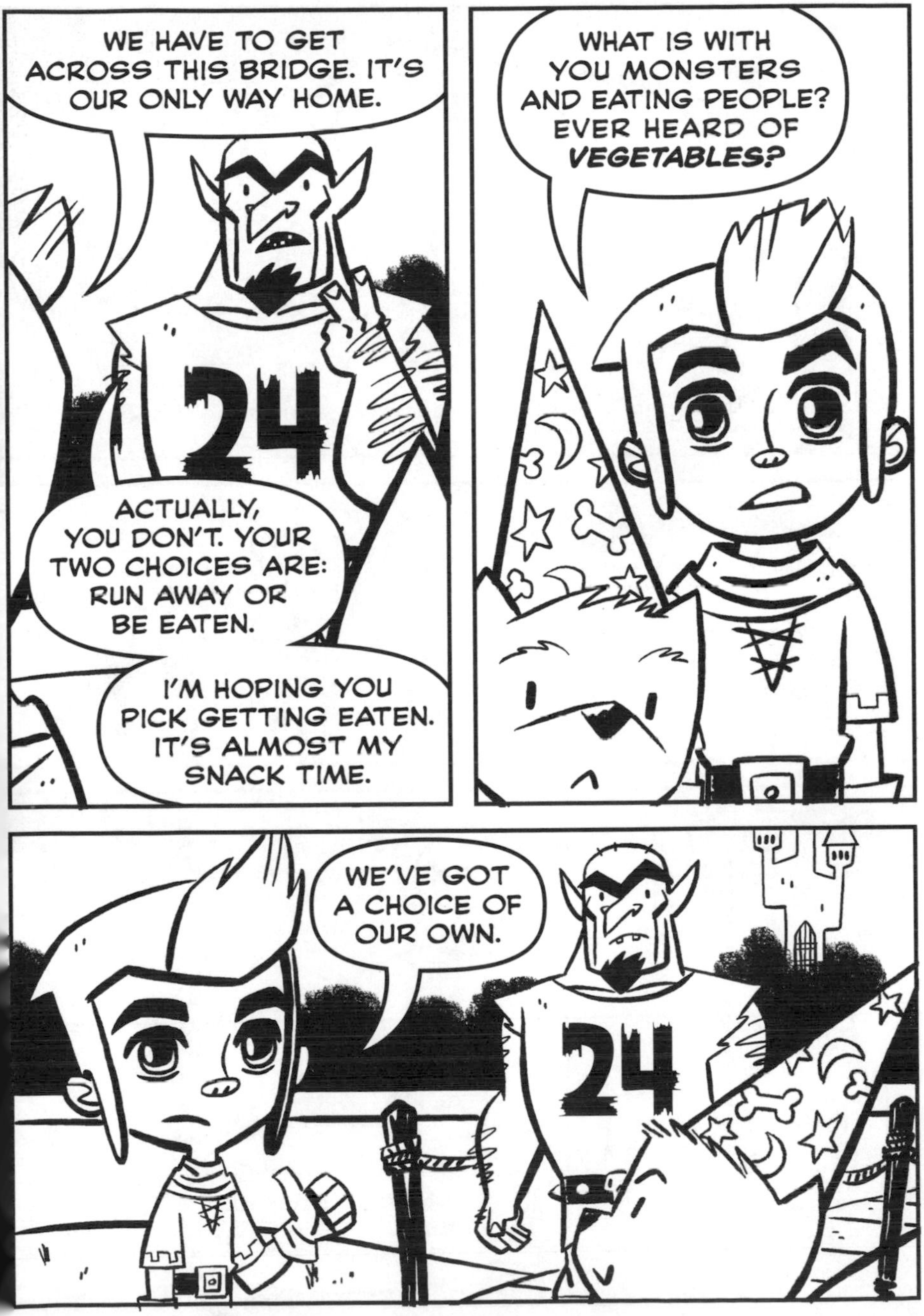
WE HAVE TO GET ACROSS THIS BRIDGE. IT'S OUR ONLY WAY HOME.
ACTUALLY, YOU DON'T. YOUR TWO CHOICES ARE: RUN AWAY OR BE EATEN.
I'M HOPING YOU PICK GETTING EATEN. IT'S ALMOST MY SNACK TIME.
WHAT IS WITH YOU MONSTERS AND EATING PEOPLE? EVER HEARD OF *VEGETABLES?*
WE'VE GOT A CHOICE OF OUR OWN.

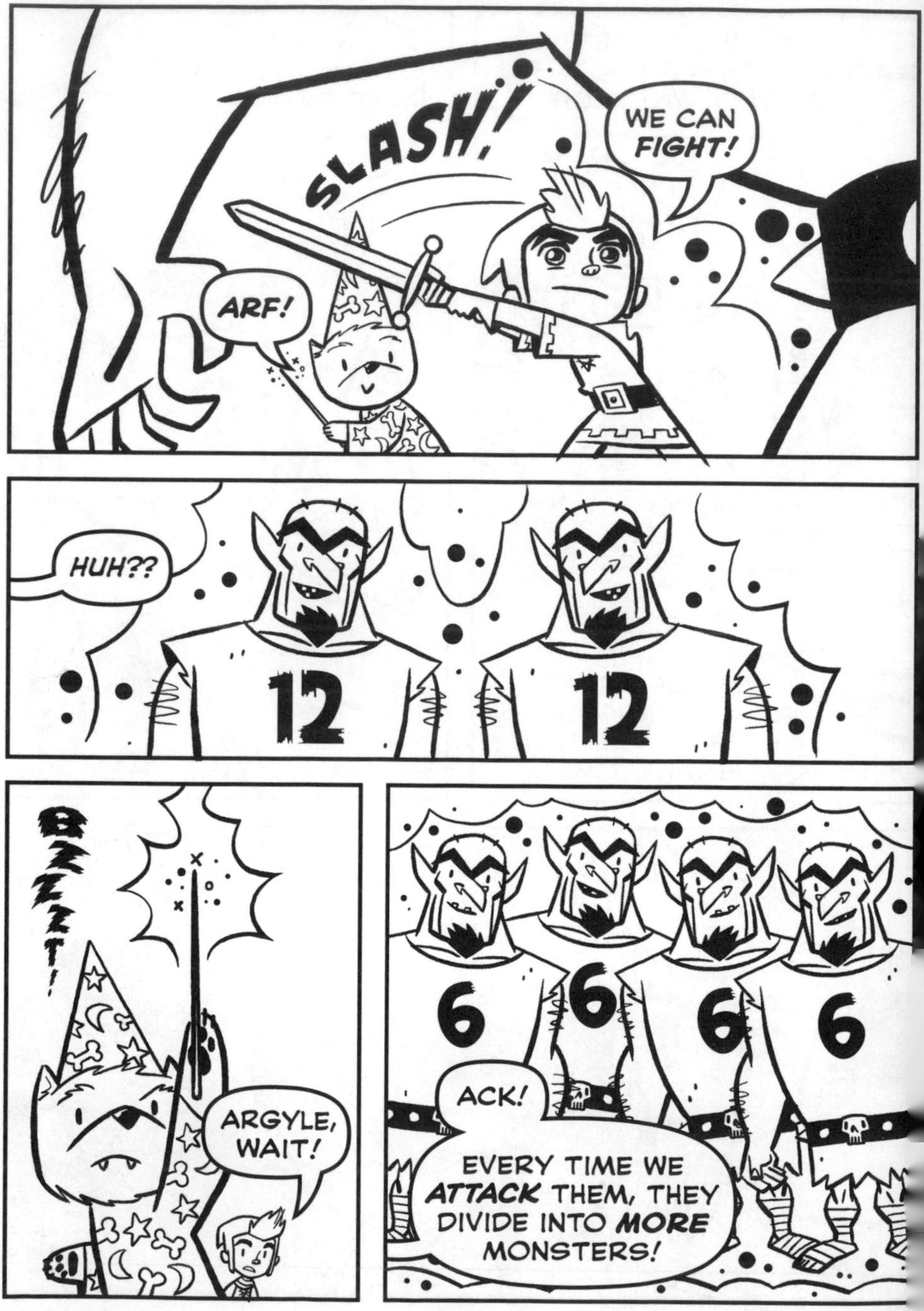
SLASH!
WE CAN FIGHT!
ARF!
HUH??
12
12
BZZZT!
ARGYLE, WAIT!
6
6
6
6
ACK!
EVERY TIME WE ATTACK THEM, THEY DIVIDE INTO MORE MONSTERS!

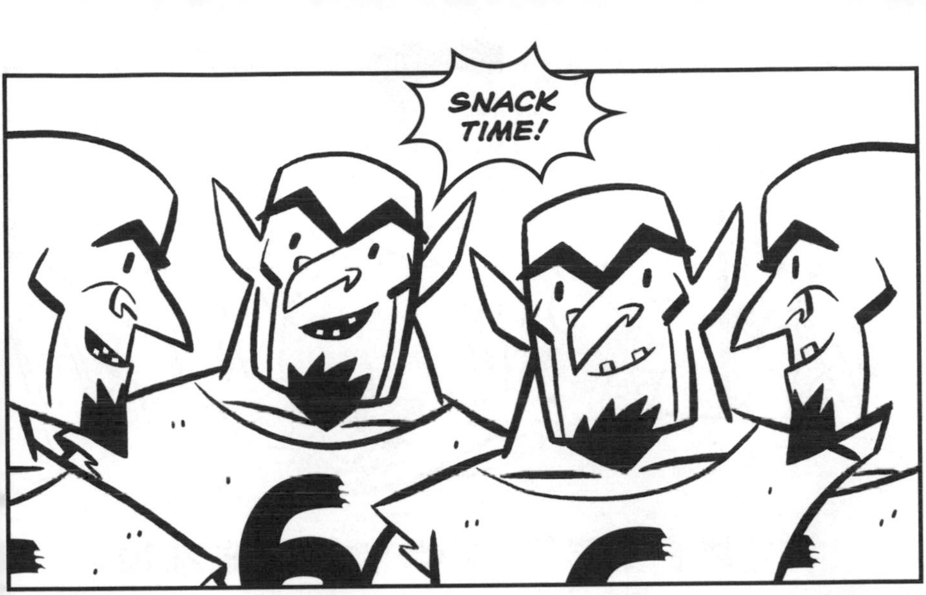
SNACK TIME!

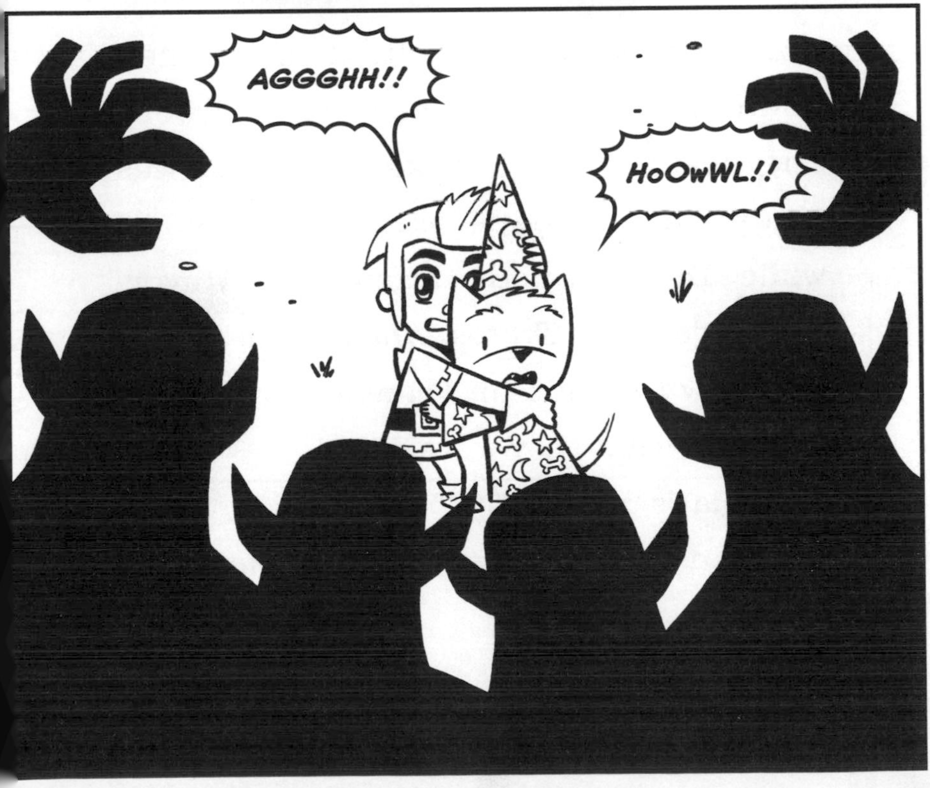
AGGGHH!!
HoOwWL!!

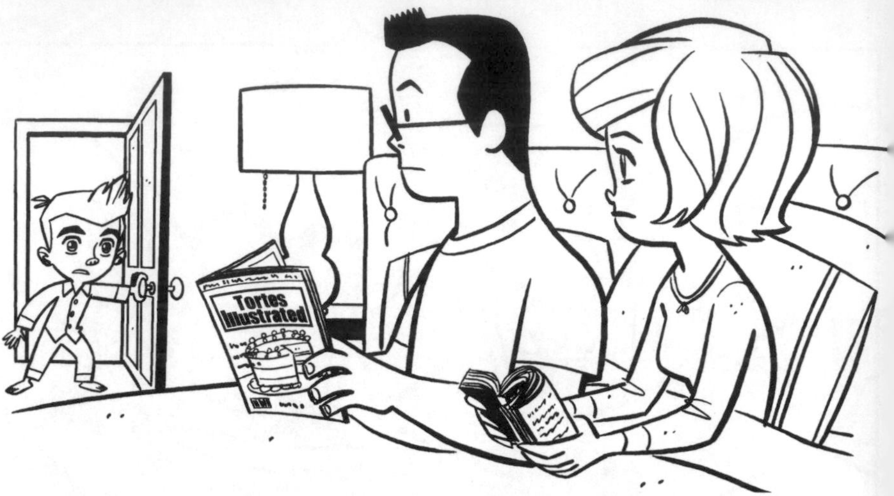
Tortes Illustrated

CHAPTER FOURTEEN

Frankie woke with a jolt, then stormed down the hall into his parents' bedroom. They were already tucked in. Mom was reading an old paperback mystery novel while Dad flipped through his favorite magazine, *Tortes Illustrated*. When they saw the look on Frankie's face, they dropped what they were doing.

"What's up, buddy?" said Dad.

"I can't believe you did this to me!" said Frankie.

"What are you talking about?" said Mom.

"I tried to study all weekend," said Frankie. "But you guys made me do other stuff that was more fun!"

"You're angry at us for having fun?" said Mom.

"No, I'm angry at you for not helping me! I'm going to fail my math quiz tomorrow!"

"Are you sure about that?" said Dad. "What's 48 divided by 4?"

"How should I kn—" The cupcake pan popped into Frankie's head. "12?"

"Right," said Mom. "And what's 50% of $2.40?"

Frankie could picture the supermarket coupons. "$1.20."

"How about 56 divided by 7?" said Dad.

Frankie pretended he was playing Kenny's new version of Yugimon. "8."

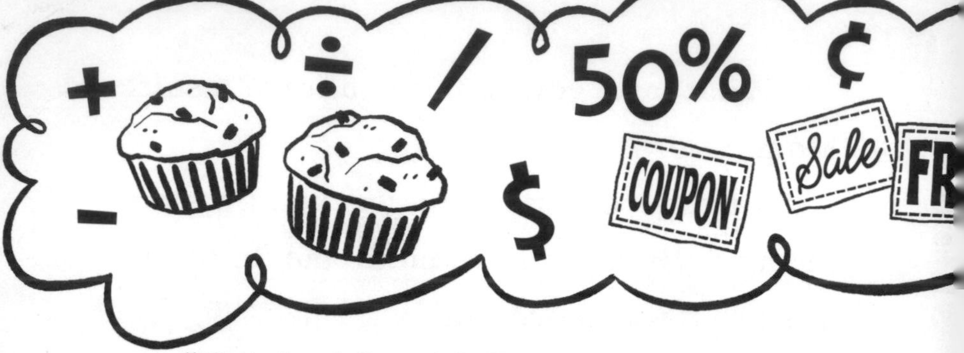
50%
COUPON
Sale
FR

"Not bad," said Piper as she poked her head into the room. "Try 348,729,561 times 0."

Frankie had to think about that one. No matter how many points a touchdown was worth, if he never scored, it would still be . . . "0!" Frankie's face lit up. "Hang on, you mean to tell me that you guys were helping me study the whole time?"

"Yep," said Dad.

"Math isn't just about crunching numbers or taking quizzes," said Piper. "It can be used for fun stuff too."

"The answers were inside you the whole time," said Mom. "We thought if we showed

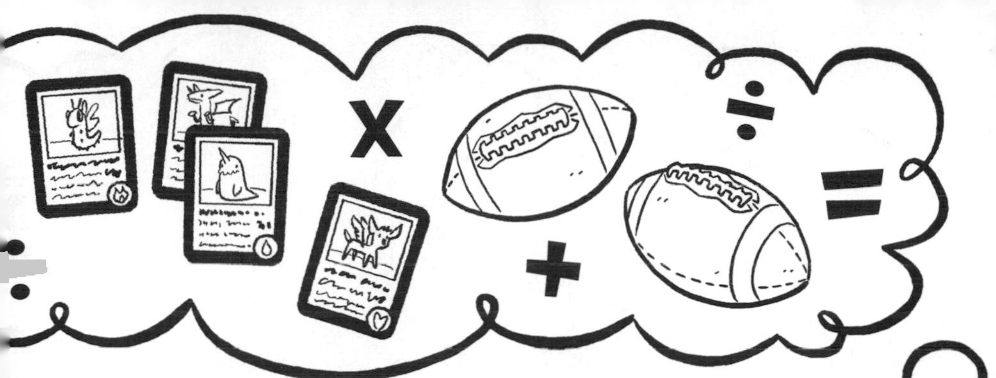

you how good you are at math in the real world, you would be more confident about passing your quiz."

Frankie had to admit, he *was* feeling pretty good about all the math he knew.

"So you really think I'll be ready?" he said.

Dad smiled and said, "We're counting on it."

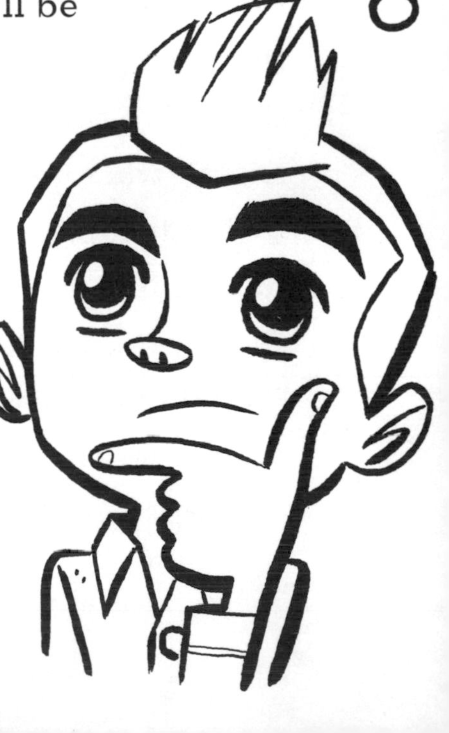

CHAPTER FIFTEEN

Frankie never could have imagined he'd be this excited to take a math quiz. But when the end of the day came on Monday, that's exactly what he was.

The feeling didn't last long. Excitement turned into nervousness as Miss Gordon slid the quiz in front of him. She reminded Frankie that he would have thirty minutes to complete it.

Frankie started to write his name at

the top of the paper. The pencil slipped in his sweaty grip, breaking the tip! His heart did jumping jacks. He glanced at the clock. A minute had already been wasted. Only twenty-nine left. This was going to be impos—!

Huh. The first problem didn't seem so bad. In fact, Frankie knew the answer just by looking at it. He scanned the rest of the quiz. The other numbers weren't so scary either.

Frankie sucked in a chest full of air and blew it out. His heart stopped beating so fast. He wiped his hands on his jeans, then he dug through his pencil box for a new weapon.

It was time to return to Arithmecca.

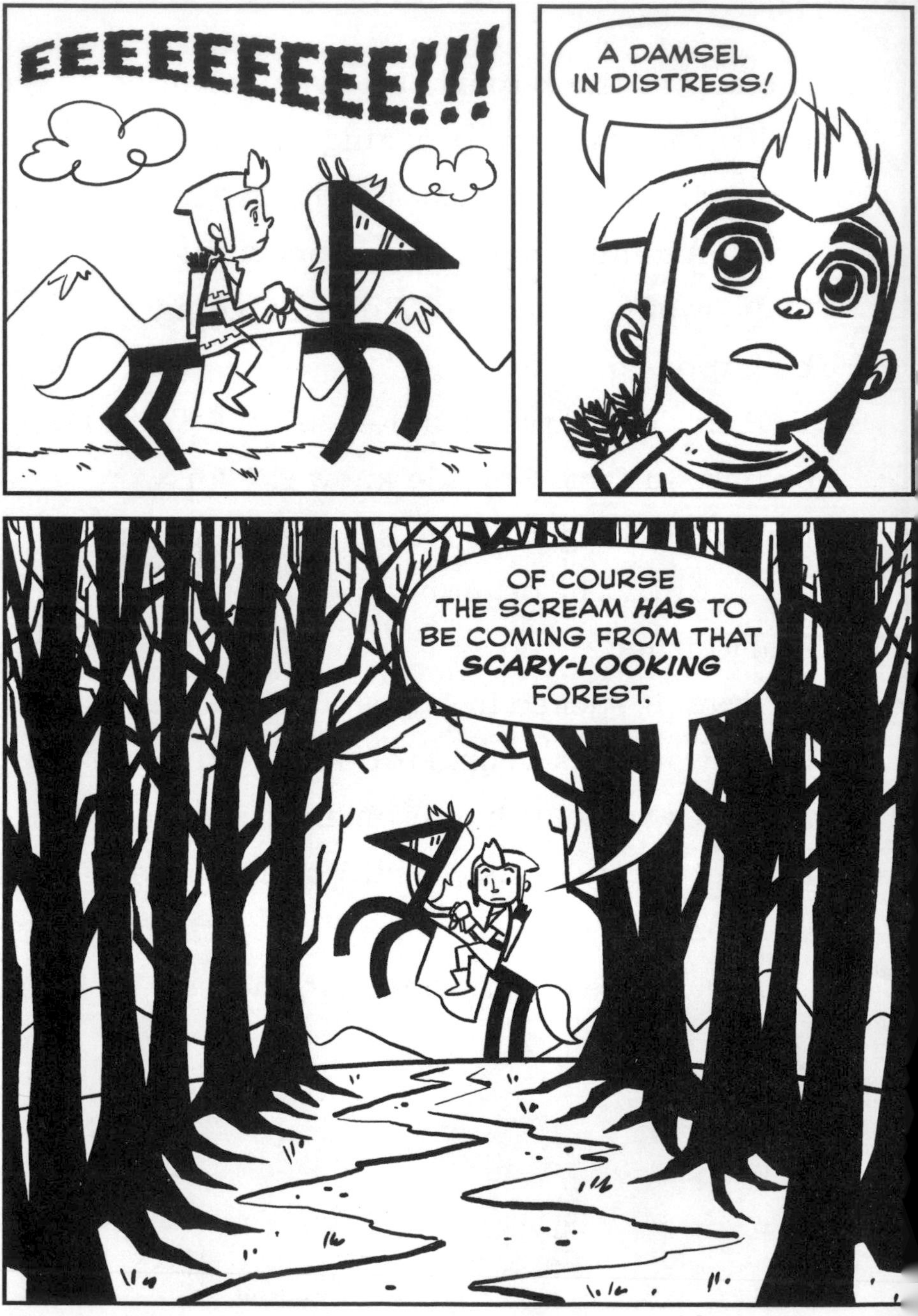
EEEEEEEEEEEE!!!
A DAMSEL IN DISTRESS!
OF COURSE THE SCREAM *HAS* TO BE COMING FROM THAT *SCARY-LOOKING* FOREST.

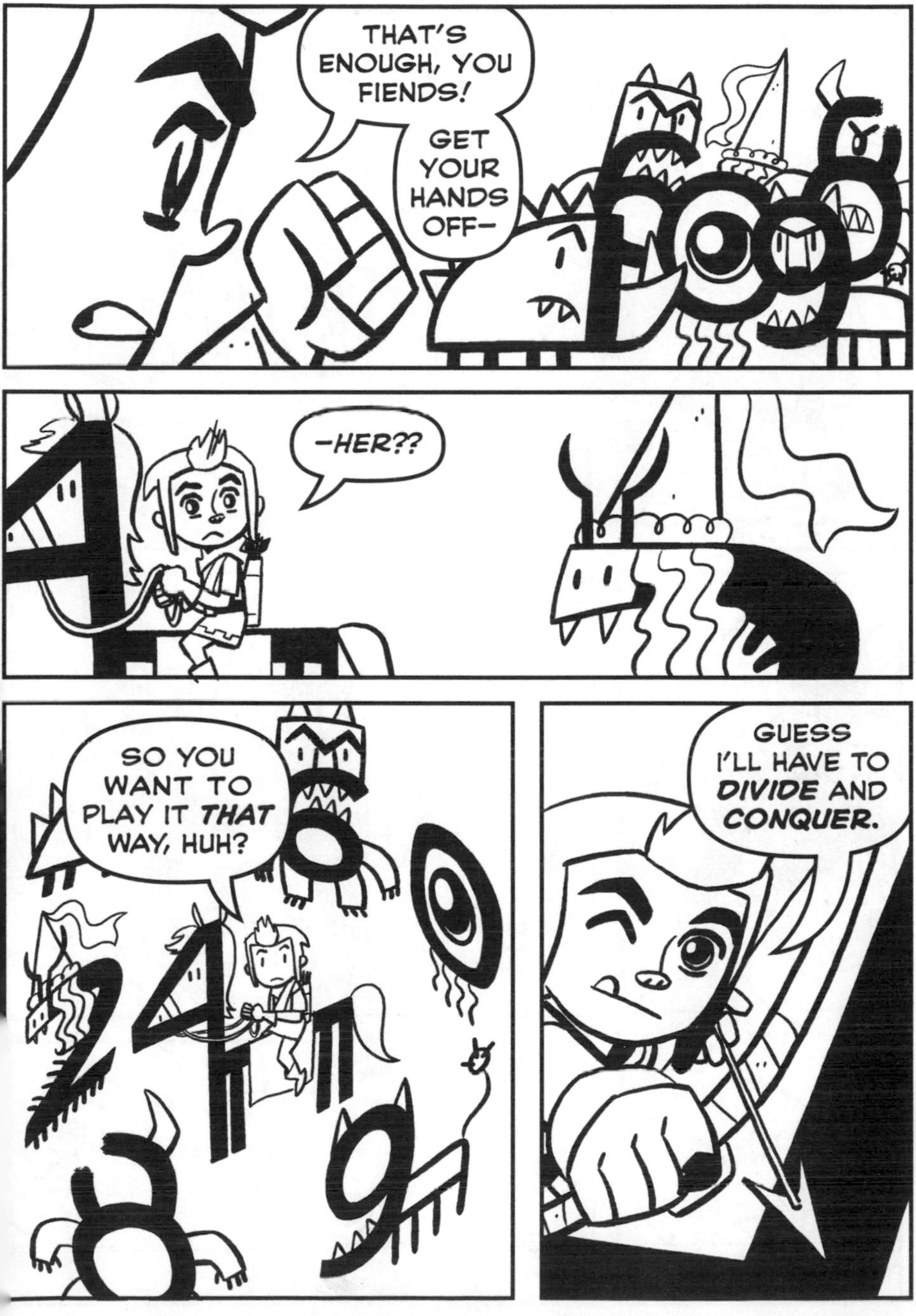
THAT'S ENOUGH, YOU FIENDS!
GET YOUR HANDS OFF—
—HER??
SO YOU WANT TO PLAY IT *THAT* WAY, HUH?
GUESS I'LL HAVE TO *DIVIDE* AND *CONQUER.*

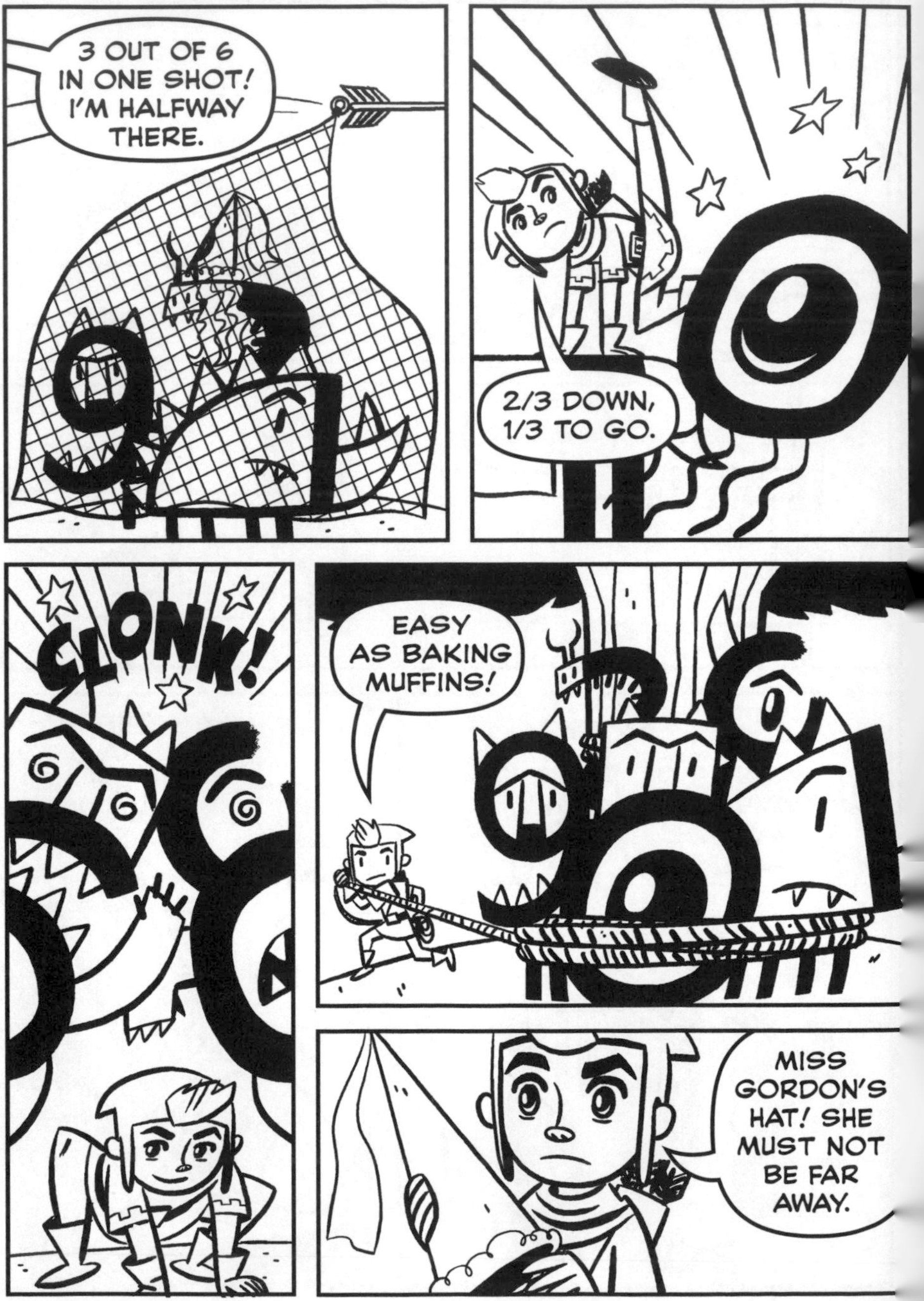

3 OUT OF 6 IN ONE SHOT! I'M HALFWAY THERE.
2/3 DOWN, 1/3 TO GO.
CLONK!
EASY AS BAKING MUFFINS!
MISS GORDON'S HAT! SHE MUST NOT BE FAR AWAY.

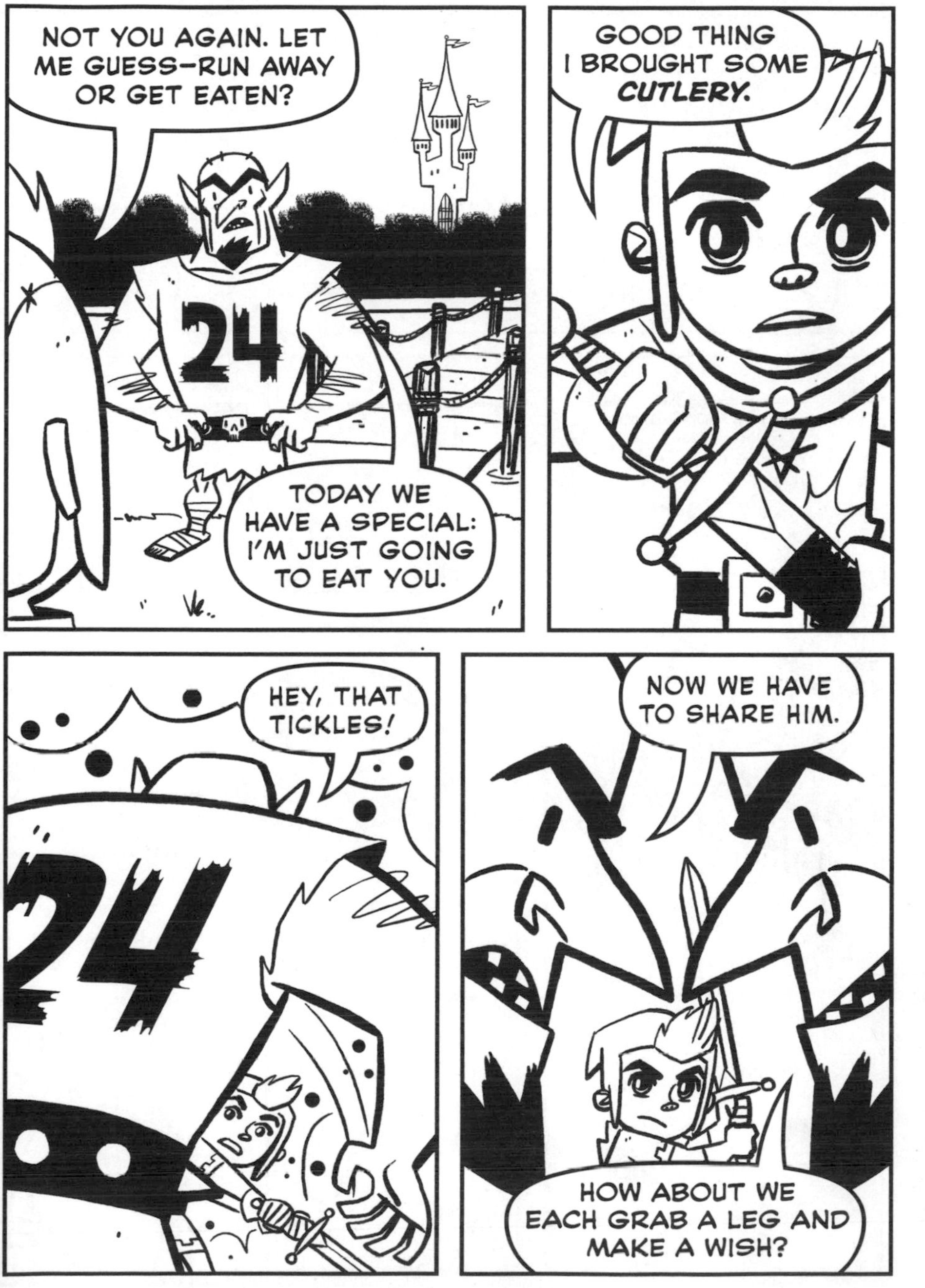
NOT YOU AGAIN. LET ME GUESS—RUN AWAY OR GET EATEN?
TODAY WE HAVE A SPECIAL: I'M JUST GOING TO EAT YOU.
GOOD THING I BROUGHT SOME *CUTLERY.*
HEY, THAT TICKLES!
NOW WE HAVE TO SHARE HIM.
HOW ABOUT WE EACH GRAB A LEG AND MAKE A WISH?

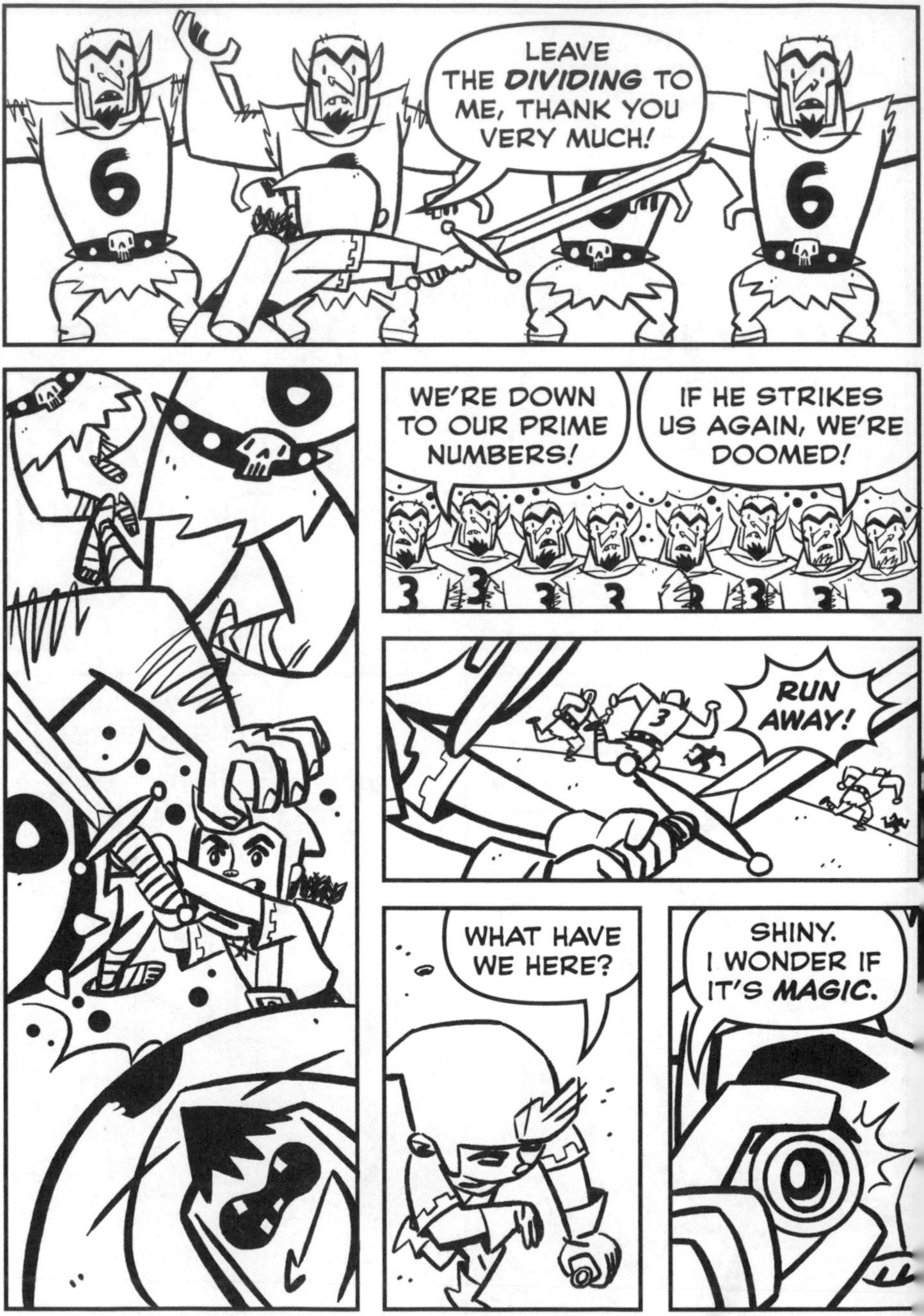
LEAVE THE *DIVIDING* TO ME, THANK YOU VERY MUCH!
6
6
WE'RE DOWN TO OUR PRIME NUMBERS!
IF HE STRIKES US AGAIN, WE'RE DOOMED!
3
RUN AWAY!
WHAT HAVE WE HERE?
SHINY. I WONDER IF IT'S *MAGIC*.

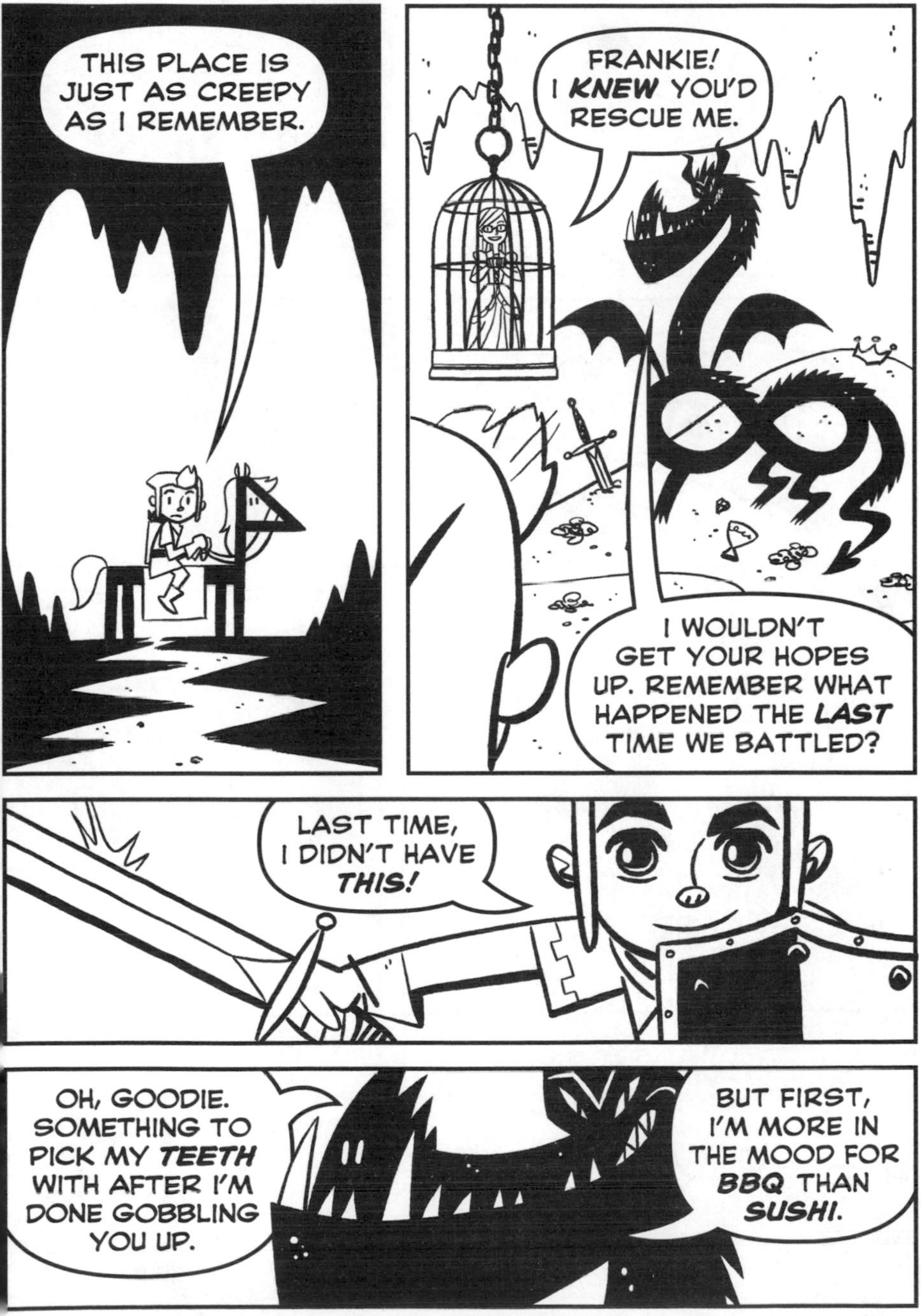
THIS PLACE IS JUST AS CREEPY AS I REMEMBER.
FRANKIE! I *KNEW* YOU'D RESCUE ME.
I WOULDN'T GET YOUR HOPES UP. REMEMBER WHAT HAPPENED THE *LAST* TIME WE BATTLED?
LAST TIME, I DIDN'T HAVE *THIS!*
OH, GOODIE. SOMETHING TO PICK MY *TEETH* WITH AFTER I'M DONE GOBBLING YOU UP.
BUT FIRST, I'M MORE IN THE MOOD FOR *BBQ* THAN *SUSHI*.

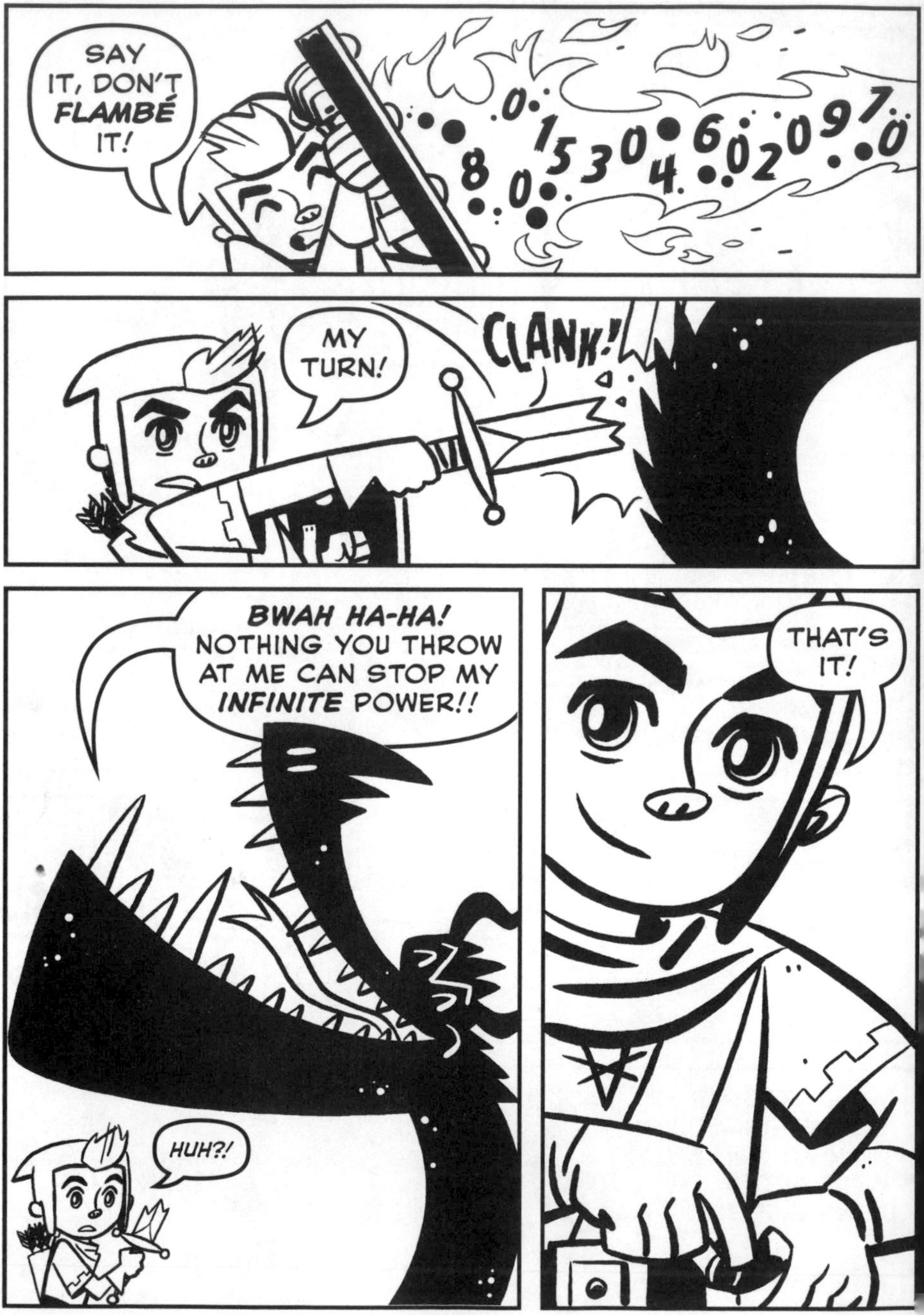
SAY IT, DON'T FLAMBÉ IT!
8 0 1 5 3 0 4 6 0 2 0 9 7 0
MY TURN!
CLANK!
BWAH HA-HA! NOTHING YOU THROW AT ME CAN STOP MY INFINITE POWER!!
HUH?!
THAT'S IT!

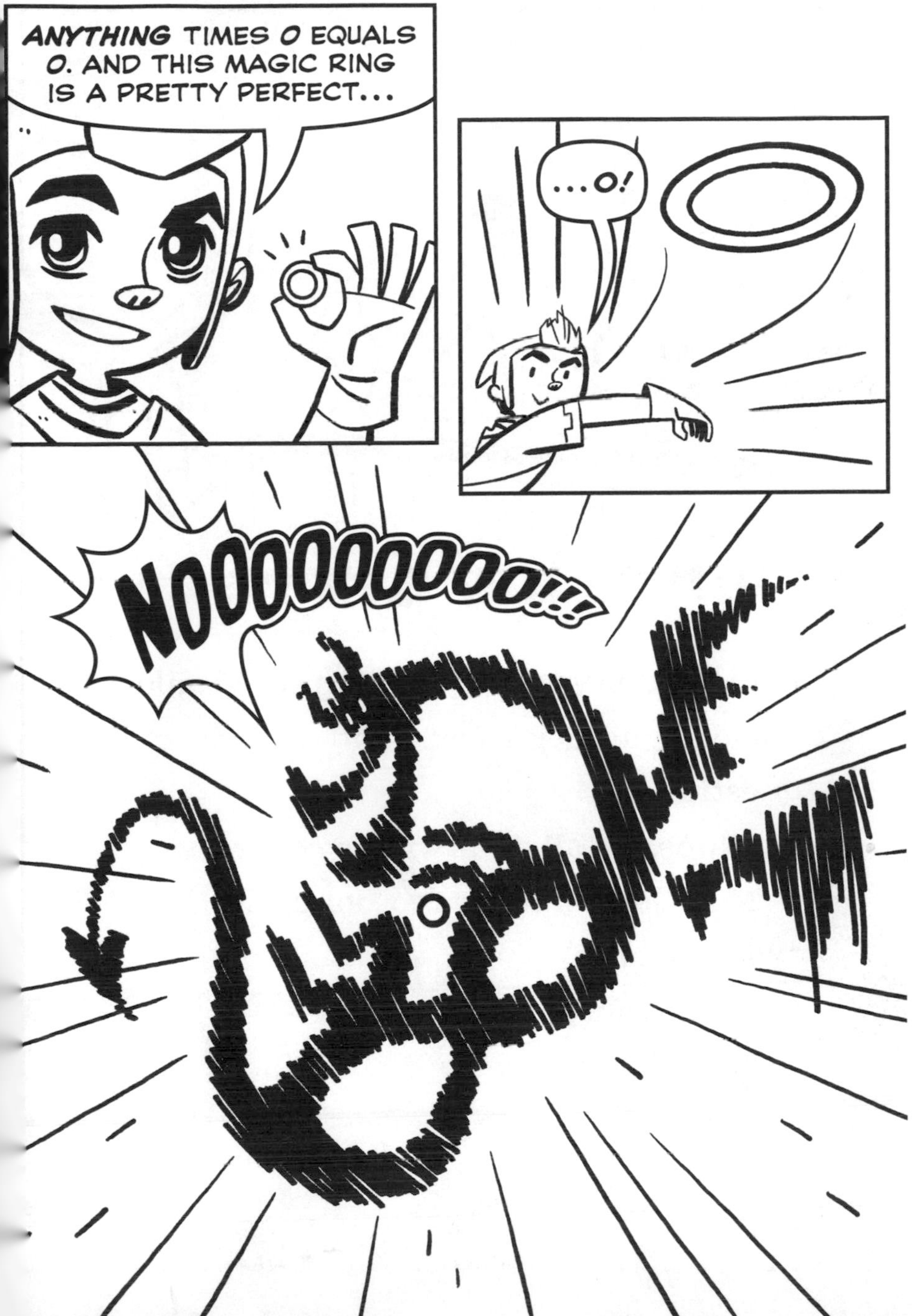
ANYTHING TIMES 0 EQUALS 0. AND THIS MAGIC RING IS A PRETTY PERFECT...
...0!
NOOOOOOOOO!!!

CHAPTER SIXTEEN

Miss Gordon was surprised to see Frankie standing at her desk. "Did you have a question?"

"Nope. I'm all done with my quiz."

Miss Gordon turned to look at the clock. "You still have—"

"Ten minutes to spare."

"Would you like to double-check your answers?"

"I already did." Frankie smiled confidently.

Miss Gordon returned the smile. "Okay, then. If you don't mind waiting, I can grade it for you now."

"Um . . . sure." Finishing the quiz was such a relief that Frankie hadn't considered how nervous he would get once it was being graded. He returned to his seat and watched carefully as Miss Gordon took a thick red pen out from her desk drawer, uncapped it, and began making marks ALL OVER HIS QUIZ.

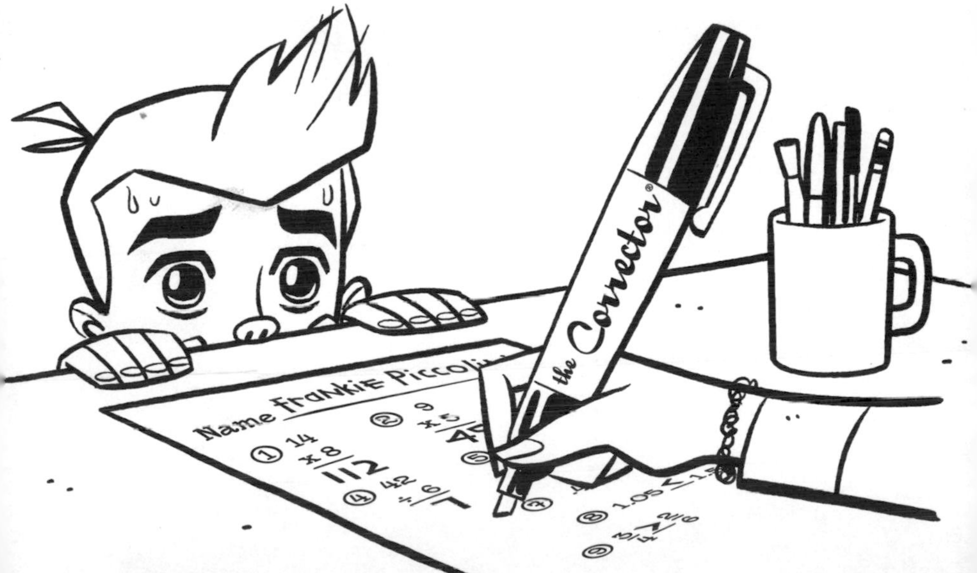
the Corrector
Name Frankie Piccolini

What was she doing? Those couldn't *all* be wrong answers. Could they?

"All done," said Miss Gordon, clicking the cap onto her pen.

Frankie slowly made his way back to Miss Gordon's desk. His legs were so wobbly, it almost felt like he had forgotten how to walk. He picked up the graded quiz with sweaty, trembling hands. His eyes were shut. He was too afraid to look. Sucking in his breath, he slowly glanced down, then opened his eyes.

CHAPTER SEVENTEEN

Frankie stared at Miss Gordon in total shock. He had aced his math quiz! The marks Miss Gordon had made were stars and smiley faces and exclamation points next to his correct answers. His paper was covered with them.

Without even stopping to say good-bye, Frankie barreled out of school for the carpool line. His family was already waiting there in Dad's SUV. Kenny was in the back-seat too.

Frankie
A+
① 14 x 8 112
② x 5 45
③ x 72
④ 42 ÷ 6 7
⑤ 35 ÷ 7 5
⑥ 54 ÷ 9 6
AWESOME!
⑦ .45 ≥ .045
GREAT JOB!
⑧ 1.05 ≤ 1.50
⑨ 3/4 ≥ 2/6
⑩ 4/8 = 3/6

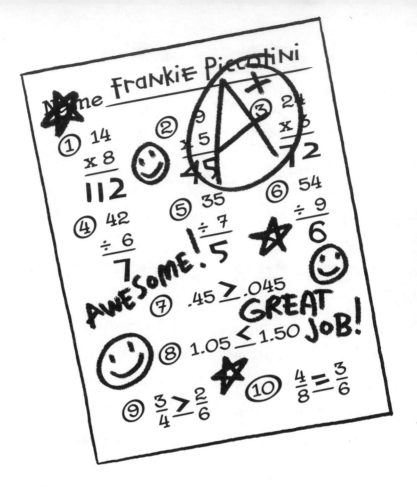

Frankie couldn't wait until he got in the car to share his good news. He held up his quiz for them to see. Everyone screamed. Dad honked his horn. Pretty soon the cars behind him started honking too. But that might have been more because Dad was blocking the exit.

To celebrate, Mom and Dad treated everyone to Mama Luigi's, the best pizzeria in town. They toasted Frankie's success with a round of grape soda.

Mom reached into her purse, and pulled out a small package wrapped in tin foil. "This was well earned," she said, handing it to Frankie.

"What's th—?" said Frankie. He tore it open. "THE NEW CAPTAIN ATOMIC COMIC BOOK!" He was so excited about passing his quiz that he had completely forgotten about it. "How did you find it?"

Dad smiled. "Let's just say that between your mother and I, we've been to about every grocery store and comic-book shop in town."

As if his night couldn't get any better,

out came Mama Luigi's famous pepperoni-and-green-olive pie. But there was a problem. Frankie, Piper, Mom, Dad, and Kenny were all eating pizza, but there were only 8 slices.

"Guess we can't split it evenly," said Piper.

"I've got this," said Frankie. Borrowing a pizza cutter, he divided each piece into 5 parts, making 40 slices. "8 for each of us."

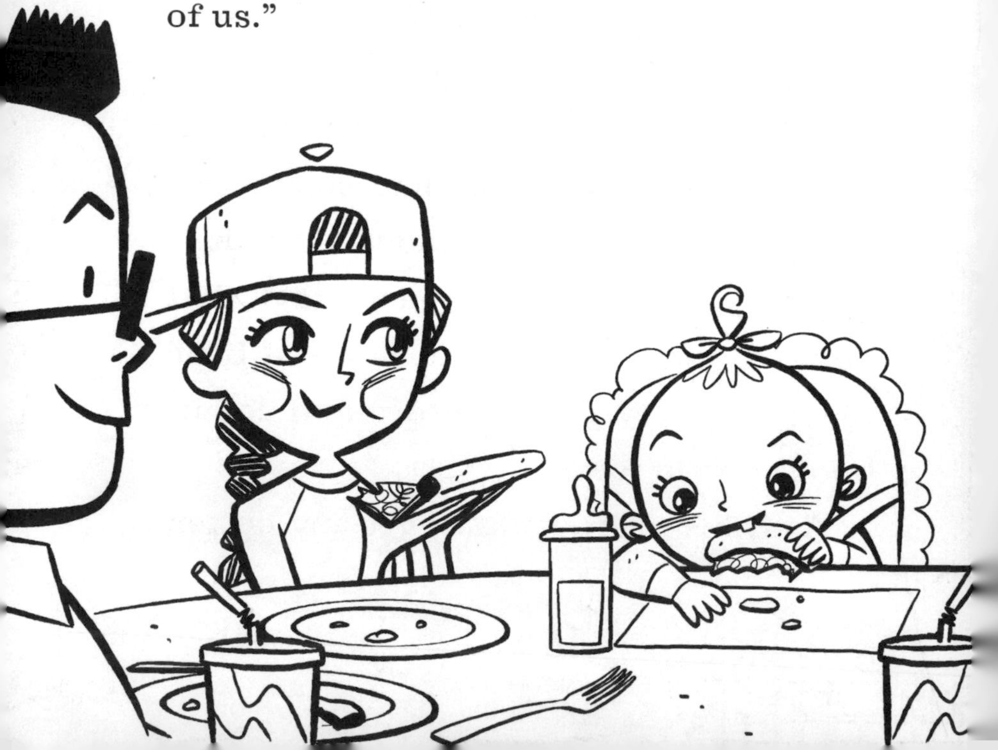

It didn't take long for those slices to disappear. Even Lucy got to gnaw on some crust. Good times were had by all.

"Now do you believe me that math is important?" said Dad.

"Sometimes," Frankie said with a mouthful of pizza, "it can even be delicious."

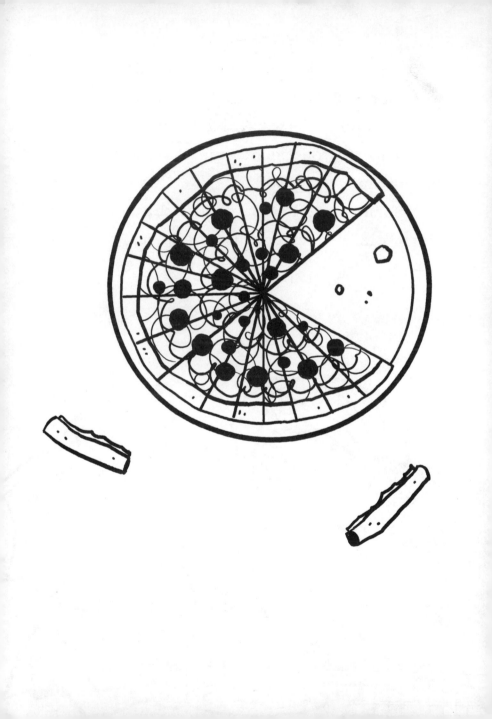

ABOUT THE CREATOR

Eric Wight spent his childhood wishing for superpowers. When that didn't pan out, he decided to learn how to write and draw. And while he may never fly or shoot lasers from his fingertips, getting to tell stories and make people laugh for a living is pretty cool too.

Maybe his wish came true after all.

Check out all the fun he's having at

ericwight.com.

TRAVEL BACK IN TIME TO HATCH FRANKIE PICKLE'S NEXT ADVENTURE!

FRANKIE PICKLE™ AND THE LAND OF THE LOST RECESS

Simon & Schuster
Books for Young Readers